Anthropocene
 by Dean Gessie

UnCollected Press

Anthropocene

Copyright © 2020 Dean Gessie
All rights reserved. This book in full form may not be used or reproduced by electronic or mechanical means without permission in writing from the author and UnCollected Press.

Book Design by UnCollected Press
Cover Art: Self-Portrait Ribbon of Darkness
Copyright © 2020 Henry G. Stanton

UnCollected Press
8320 Main Street, 2nd Floor
Ellicott City, MD 21043

For more books by UnCollected Press:
www.therawartreview.com

First Edition 2020
ISBN: 978-1-71613-795-2

This collection of stories
is dedicated to my wife, Julie,
my daughter, Katya,
and my son, Sacha.
My gratitude for our family
is an uncountable number.

Contents

Head Smashed in Buffalo Jump 1
Nobody Knows How Much You Love Him 7
The Red-eye from Guernica to Pamplona 12
Officers of Adaptation to Climate Change 17
Gods, Titans and Junk 24
Empire in the Gardens of Babylon 31
Hoodwinked 42
Blaming Justin Bieber 49
Necropsy 56
An Infinite Game 63
Cicada 67
A Night at the Oprah [sic] 73
Dakhma 78
Dementia 86
(Hogtied Girl) 90
The Brief, Sad Tale of Ping Pong 93
The Intervention 100
La Cuenta, por favor 108
Misanthropes 111
Extinction Redux 118
Gloria in Excelsis Deo 122
1/32nd African American 127
Amerika [sic] 133

Head Smashed in Buffalo Jump

When Saanvi was born, her father purchased a tree to plant in the backyard. He went from one nursery to another like a pollinating bee. He was drawn to a young *Betula nigra* or river birch with its light taupe outer skin and salmon and cinnamon beneath. A salesman said, "The bark changes from flaky strips to thick plates." He added, cryptically, as it were, "The tree grows with the family."

Digging to commemorate his daughter's birthday, Parminder struck a gas line with his pickaxe and cleared the neighbourhood. While the firemen did their work, his eight-year-old son, Rajeev, introduced his father to sibling rivalry. "Why," he said, "didn't I get a tree?" The question was a long rod pushed through a gutted animal hung over an open fire.

One year to the day, Saanvi died of cot death and for inexplicable reasons. Her mother had not smoked. The baby slept on its side. There were no soft objects in the crib. The family doctor shook his head dolefully and tendered a diagnosis of murder: "Perhaps," he said, "it is God's will." In any event, Saanvi looked like a porcelain doll and this made her death all the more galling. For her parents, competing impulses of devotion and austerity had come a cropper.

In the aftermath, a hallway lamp was left on to light the way for the departed soul. Food was vegetarian and without onion or garlic. The river birch was decorated with Saanvi's baby clothes and months of heretofore digital photos, each date-stamped with foreboding. Parminder put his arm around his son's shoulders and said, "This is why you didn't get a tree." It was the beginning of a new habit for Parminder, spitting like a cobra, and Rajeev, the remainder of the quotient, was often a target.

Annaliese, Saanvi's mother, understood the cold trail of cause of death to be proof of her own culpability. When no one is to blame, the mother is always to blame. Her statement of fact was paradoxical but obviously self-incriminatory: "I did not see," she said, "when my daughter cried out." Be that as it may, Annaliese experienced ownership of Saanvi's death as a kind of lobotomy. She was left emotionally blunted and the complexity of psychical life had become a singularity.

After the mourning period of thirteen days, Parminder stripped the river birch of its baby clothes and photos and picked at its outer layer of curling, paper-thin scales until his own fingers bled. He then turned and held up his hands to his wife in a gesture of unambiguous bloody surrender. No one would age with this tree. Time had stopped.

But the birds had other ideas. At three o'clock in the morning, Parminder was awakened by the sound of rustling in the wind. For her part, Annaliese heard a mechanical rumble that was typically too low-pitched for the human ear, the *infrasound* of shaking tails. To this was soon added a screech and another and a caterwaul that was precisely the tone of Saanvi's cry. As Annaliese threw off her bed sheets, her eyebrows lifted hopefully. She would not overlook her daughter's cry a second time.

At the window and over his wife's shoulder, Parminder surveyed the scene with bitter reproach. Roosting in his river tree was a muster of peacocks. Of course, his battle with these birds had been going on since the beginning of time. He called them the *adversaries* or the *devils* or the *enemy*. They were forever on neighbourhood rooves or underfoot, mewling and shitting and mating and obscuring welcome mats with their nests. City officials ignored his demands to relocate or poison the fowl. And now, of course, these speakers of tongues were mimicking the cry of his own dead daughter to taunt him in his sleep. Parminder, the cobra, longed to spit in the eyespots of each and every peacock tail.

But the birds were a great comfort to Annaliese. She believed the peacocks to be the reincarnated soul of her dead daughter, each cry of the bird/child evidence of what she described – fitfully, it seemed – as *transmigration*. As a result, she rose each morning with the infrasound of the bird tails and sat naked in front of the window and before her easel and art supplies. She would continue as she had done with Saanvi, sketch the greatest object of beauty she had ever seen. Parminder would waken later to the wailing of the enemy, each cry a multi-barbed hook that hoisted him dockside.

The idea of a prescribed burn came from city officials and the six o'clock news. He was refused a permit to remove or cut down his own tree and told, ostensibly, that only an act of God trumped local ordinances against free will. That same day, Parminder watched news reports of the destruction of Fort McMurray by a wildfire the size and intensity of a thousand suns. If the army could evacuate 88,000 people, then, surely, he could speed the relocation of forty or fifty peacocks. The birds amplified his suffering and they must be defeated.

    Even so, he was conflicted as to whether or not his plan was an act of mercy or revenge. He was comfortable with the satisfaction of either and got neither. He brought Annaliese with him to the self-serve gas on King Street. They bought two jerry cans. He filled one. She filled one. Later that afternoon, they carried the cans into the backyard and set them down in the shade of the river birch. Parminder then went to the storage shed and retrieved two large aerosol containers he typically filled with crabgrass killer. He filled one with gas. She filled the other.

    Parminder instructed Annaliese to spray the hairy twigs and the dark green leaves. He, himself, would address the thickening plates of bark between him and his dead daughter. Anyway, the fire released a mushroom plume of smoke followed by a wisp, much like the camouflaged exit of a genie from a magic lantern. Said Parminder, evoking an emotional settlement, "This is for my pain and suffering. And," he added, carefully redacting rage, bargaining and depression, "so that you may move quickly from denial to acceptance." His wife's response was a flower of silk or tissue, both precious and disappointing. "Oh," she whispered.

    When he opened his eyes before first light that morning, Annaliese was already at the window dragging a burnt willow stick over newsprint. Through the ribs of the chair, he saw her straight back, long, black hair and pancaked buttocks. He blinked with grudging comprehension as he listened to the cries of his daughter. These were surely bubbles of remembrance beneath the sea. He would surface and breathe and they, like the peacocks, would be gone.

    But the birds had other ideas. They had populated the charred limbs of the tree, as per usual. They shook out their tails and continued to cry out in the voice of Saanvi. These birds and that stricken birch described perfectly the bereft, end-of-world setting of Parminder's heart and the consolations for his wife of imagination and homage or, to hear Parminder, fruits of the poisonous tree. He was disconsolate as he gazed upon his wife's breasts. They held no interest.

Parminder needed a different plan, but he was flummoxed. How might he justify extermination of the enemy and sidestep both social excommunication and stiff fines from the city? Those closest to his location described the river birch as the Tree of Singh, aural equivalent to apocalyptic hellfire. These good neighbours were sympathetic and would look the other way. Those further from his location described the river birch as the Tree of Singh, a producer of podcasts of pastoral poems. These bad neighbours would cry for human blood if his coup did not have a leg to stand on.

But they were not alone in the house and neglect made a foursome. Rajeev was at the door in his pajamas. "I can't sleep," he said, screwing the balls of his fists into his eyes. "It's the peacocks. It's always the peacocks." Annaliese continued with her sketch, sussing out elusive lines of perspective, while Parminder spat angrily, "Your mother is naked! How *dare* you come here and use such language!" Rajeev burst into tears and ran back to his room.

But Rajeev's tears were not an isolated shower. Three days later, Parminder responded to a knock at the front door and discovered his son in the company of his teacher. Rajeev was only sniffling at the moment but the blue sacks beneath his brown eyes suggested a deep and protracted trauma. Miss Rachael had accompanied Rajeev on the school bus, both to comfort him and to provide context to his parents.

"The field trip, I'm afraid, was not a good experience."

Parminder said, "I have no idea what you're talking about."

Miss Rachael surfaced a pamphlet from her handbag and gave it to Parminder. Apparently, the whole class had gone to a museum called, Head Smashed in Buffalo Jump. Mrs. Singh had signed the forms.

"We were there to learn about Indigenous peoples, how they used to harvest buffalo by driving them over a cliff."

Parminder did not blame his son for walking in on his naked mother or using a profane word. He held him close to his legs to champion his cause. "And this is what passes for education in this country? You expose young children to this barbaric practice?"

This was a topic for secondary school and Miss Rachael was loathe to debate.

"It was a different time, Mr. Singh."

Parminder read from the pamphlet, "*Then, at full gallop, the buffalo would fall from the weight of the herd pressing behind them, breaking their legs and rendering them immobile.*"

"The hunt met physical, emotional and spiritual needs."

"*After falling off the cliff, the injured buffalo were finished off by other warriors at the cliff base armed with spears and clubs.*"

"It's a UNESCO World Heritage Site."

"And no one asks any questions about the pain and suffering of those poor animals waiting for death and without a leg to stand on?" Parminder's indignation was briefly interrupted by a peculiar feeling of déjà vu.

Miss Rachael answered his question with a kind of sealed affidavit. "We don't get to judge the history and culture of colonized peoples."

Parminder's eyes bulged with apoplexy. He wondered if his own brown skin belonged on a list of invisible things. In any event, the seed of an idea was planted. It grew in the shade of a black river birch and it smelled of exculpation. He closed the door on Miss Rachael and said to his son, now that they were alone, "Where were all those tears when your sister died?"

Very early the next morning, Parminder dreamed of the buffalo runners. Each was cloaked in the skin of a coyote or wolf. They pursued their quarry into drive lanes with dozens of cairns to either side. Parminder heard the snorts of the beasts and the crashing of their hooves. As they came to the cliff's edge, those in the front were betrayed by the momentum of those in the rear, jostled and jolted and toppled and pitched.

At the bottom of the cliff was Parminder surrounded by his warrior brothers. It was his job to club the brains of the peacocks in the kill area. Effectively, the broken buffalo had become peacocks, each a twitching, screeching irregular shape of tail and claw and beak and mortification. Feathers made a kind of communal burial shroud. Peacock blood was given freely.

When Parminder got out of bed, he whispered in his wife's direction, "We will save souls tonight." And then he went into the basement to retrieve his air rifle and a few boxes of led pellets. He opened the window onto the street light and the dead tree of his heart and settled into a crouch beneath the pane. He believed it was his birthright to speed the migration of his daughter's soul to a higher plane or, failing that, to separate his wife from belief in that kind of nonsense. It was a short hop from zealot to heretic and he would be comfortable with the satisfaction of either.

The killing of the birds was rather easy. Each arrived at irregular intervals and squatted at twenty-five feet in the crosshairs of a rifle that fired at 500 feet per second. Each struck the ground like a sandbag at the end of an antiquated rope and pulley. The cull was ceremony or the cull was theatre. It didn't matter. His needs and his rights were sacred. Who could judge?

He awoke much later than usual because of his work through the earliest hours of the morning and the absence of his baby daughter's cries. Because his wife was sketching at the window, his heart sank immediately with the only plausible prediction. Indeed, she did not see the carnage at the perimeter of that blighted tree. Instead, she drew peacocks crouched on fulsome green limbs in the kind of detail that only the obsessions of grief and imagination can provide.

Rajeev was at the door and whispered through the crack in the jamb, "I heard noises." He added, hesitantly, "Is mama naked?"

Parminder shot his son a look that travelled at 500 feet per second.

Nobody Knows How Much You Love Him

This is how your story begins. Your mother-in-law sings to your two-week-old son, his hairless head droll contrast to her own stacked ash layers: "*Fais dodo, Colas, mon p'tit frère. Fais dodo, t'auras du lolo.*"

We'll call that *mood,* a rosy blush in the sunroom. It leaves you completely unprepared for the *hook.* Says Claudine, "He's not breathing very well."

That catches your interest. You're out of the sunroom and out of doors, contemplating space debris. Claudine's *tone* is composed, like she's questioning the efficiency of a furnace. This is good. It confirms the text of the baby manual: *The first two weeks after a baby's birth are generally very uneventful.*

But Claudine is too clever by half, frowns, shrugs her shoulders, channels your own denial. Now, of course, neither of you is to be believed. You fear a *whopper* at the end of that hook.

Your wife appears. She's wearing the Cherry Cheetah onesie that unzips in the front for easy nursing, makes of her, she says, an *equal opportunity deployer.* Her smile is amiable but dopy, the result of sleep deprivation and a ten-pound six-ounce, graduation gift.

But a twenty-minute nap is anesthetic only, causes a reversible loss of consciousness and sensation. There will be plenty of that soon: consciousness and sensation and *terror.* We'll call that *foreshadowing.*

Afterward, you must have mentioned the *breathing thing,* because Emma immediately presses her ear close to Sebastian's nose. It's true. His breathing is shallow, but that's normal, right? You listen, too. There's a game you've learned about willing data into the shape of your own desires, the shape of a fish, a game, it seems, whose returns improve if you're the one seconding denial, frowning and shrugging your shoulders.

You say, "He sounds okay to me."

Emma says, "I think he sounds fine. What do you think?"

You say, "He sounds okay to me. We'll just keep an eye out."

Okay, now we've got *characters in a situation with a problem,* but you're dealing with it. You imagine the kinds of items that will kill this story from the get-go: bronchodilators, steroids or diuretics. Later, you can take him to the water, develop his lungs.

Claudine keeps her distance, skulks, prowls, feigns indifference. You read respect for the parents, an admirable move. Only much later do you reimagine the moment as self-preservation, her glances behind and askance like those of a wild animal fleeing dogs.

But not everyone escapes the dogs. The next day, they force you and Emma up a tree. We'll call it the *complication*. It turns out you're not blind after all. That eye you're keeping out is a compound lens, corrects and magnifies unpleasant truths. Sebastian will not nurse. The milk (*lolo*) makes a splatter sheet of his cheeks. He gasps for air almost as often as he sucks. You look at Emma; she at you. You know what you have to do. Foreboding is an iceberg on a fixed course.

*

Suspense accompanies you into the emergency room at Southlake. As short fiction goes, this one's a page-turner. *The suspense is killing you.* The triage nurse has a marked-up copy of your story. You go directly into an examination room.

The doctor's face is the emotional colour of all things kind. His kind face and his white coat are the perfect plot device: *deus ex machina*. You invest in him the powers of a beneficent god. Problem solved. Case closed.

"Thank you," you say, "for seeing our son so quickly." You imply that the doctor is making some kind of personal choice. Is it hubris or fear or imbecility?

The doctor corrects you, says, "We don't take chances with babies."

Momentarily, you think of the suffering bipeds for whom health care is roulette. You feel *self-conflicted* about the suffering bipeds, but not for long.

While the doctor looks at your son, you look at your wife. When did *she* arrive? Is it possible that she, too, has feelings for your son? You hug Emma because you need to be reintroduced. You need to be *forgiven*.

This next line is a shopworn standard from a medical drama: *We need to run some tests.*

"Something's wrong," the doctor adds. "His lips turned blue when I used the tongue depressor."

You stop listening after that. What these tests are, you have no idea. You only remember, *something's wrong*. Now, your wife, Emma, is a *sympathetic character,* her compassion a tuning fork, a pure, constant pitch. The two of you stand in the waiting room. You hug and you cry. Ironically, the air conditioning makes cold comfort of Emma's shoulder, the kind of *imagery* you get from a tearjerker. You fear it will end badly, this story of yours, that you will become parents whose loss is greater than the sum of their fears.

The seedlings in the ground are *blame*.

*

At four in the morning, traffic is light on the 404. Speedy processing in *emerge* and light traffic on the 404. *Something's wrong.*

Emma is in the ambulance with Sebastian heading toward Sick Kids in Toronto. You follow in the Dodge Sundance. The kind doctor in the white coat said, "His heart is working too hard."

It's the middle of winter and the heater in your piece-of-crap car still doesn't work. But that's not why you shiver.

And the ice on the windshield might as well be ice forming over a lake. You're beneath the surface, peering up and into a reality that is increasingly opaque, rationing your oxygen, dreaming of cremation.

You start to sob. Hunched in the car, tears drop from your lashes onto the steering wheel. Your breathing is labored. You imagine yourself an empath: *I am my son struggling for life.*

The ambulance is travelling fast. You feel obligated to remain in its slipstream. The thought occurs to you that any sudden de-acceleration on the part of the ambulance could cause a rear-end crash. You measure the lesser evil in your mind, living with the loss of your son against an end-of-times inferno for the three of you. You keep the results to yourself.

Concerns are more practical at Sick Kids. The ambulance gets the red carpet treatment. You look for parking. *You spend fifteen minutes looking for parking.* The only thought that rescues you from murderous rage is remembering that your toddler, Camille, is at home with Claudine. Your little girl is like her mother, light and breeze and a well where wishes are made and realized. *Everything will be okay.*

*

But it's not okay. This doctor reveals the results of more tests. We'll call it the *crisis*. Sebastian has coarctation of the aorta. He needs immediate surgery. You hear the rest of it through cottony walls of psychotropic drugs: *congenital heart defect* and *localized deformity of the tunica media*. You feel like an astronaut in space, one whose tether has been cut and whose oxygen is low.

The doctor says Sebastian's odds are very good. Of course, gamblers play good odds all the time. Gamblers lose more than they win. All you can think about are *action verbs*, gerunds like *cutting*, *opening*, *retracting* and *sewing*. You have no comfort zone with great odds and great verbs.

Hours are compressed into minutes. Sebastian is on a gurney on his way to the surgery theatre. An attending nurse says, "Do you want to give him a kiss?" Did you hear *final* kiss? You don't know. You press your lips against your son's cheek. Emma can't do it. You and she cry again, beside yourselves with fear. This can't be the last time you see your son alive. Hemingway might have written *that* story. You're glad Hemingway is dead.

At this point, the *setting* becomes important. The waiting room is huge, but it's not big enough for you. You top up your miles of pacing by going outside and navigating the block around the hospital. Your dress shoes are ankle deep in slush. You fill the bowl of your pipe and light it because self-harm is the least of your worries. A sinister idea enters your mind. Maybe your son's *localized deformity* is the product of your inhaling ammonia and arsenic? The seedlings of blame have found fertile ground here.

Plot twist. You discover the real enemy. You discover *religion*. You use the word *fuck* many times and it's not a pleasant conversation with God. You don't see that in popular fiction very often. Who would dare? *You* know who would dare. The Hospital for Sick Children is full of parents negotiating similar Faustian deals. In fact, you create of your lungs zeppelins of tobacco smoke, think, *take me, instead*.

Ice pellets awaken you from self-absorption. You have an *epiphany*. Your wife is suffering, alone. Apparently, the world isn't big enough for your feet and your hysteria, but your wife remains a point of light flickering in the holy of holies. This is transformative. This is *forever*. In the waiting room, you hug Emma because you need to be reintroduced. You need to be forgiven, *again*.

*

The next day, your baby becomes that astronaut in deep space, connected to life critical systems. He is lying in an adult bed with tubes attached to his side, his neck and his arm. A ventilator pumps breathable air into his lungs. He is so small that you don't even notice him when you enter the room. Emma says, "He's right *there*." Good God, it's true. He is on his side producing data for machines. He is still and alive and beautiful. The *climax* is as promised. You feel euphoric and buoyant. You feel like you're floating in the salt water of a sensory deprivation chamber. All your years as an English teacher have prepared you for this one artless moment, a moment of dissociative bliss, the legendary *happy ending*.

But don't get too comfortable. It turns out that the *denouement* is a black hole from which *Nobody* returns. It turns out that this story isn't your story, after all. In fact, it's not even your son's story or your wife's story. *Nobody* writes this story. *Nobody* takes responsibility for its structure and outcome. If it will give you closure, imagine a *ghost writer* and a different kind of sensory deprivation chamber, the horizonless, salt water of a *dead sea*. But, really, *Nobody*'s in charge and *Nobody* listens to your prayers. You've won this round, but you can't possibly win them all. So, you're best to hug your baby while you can, smell and kiss him while you can. Because *Nobody* knows how much you love him and *Nobody* gives a shit.

The Red-eye from Guernica to Pamplona

Finnegan, the greyhound, completes his backyard romp and re-enters the sliding, glass door. Marjorie and Raymond anticipate staccato panting and paw-like pontoons of mud. What they get is a pocket-sized hare in the jaws of their *rescue* from West Virginia. Small irony.

"Oh, my god," says Marjorie, a woman for whom human decency understates her own example.

Raymond, a few furlongs off the lead, but in the sweepstakes for *good head overall*, thinks his wife will be traumatized by the sight of a prey animal crushing the trachea of its prey. He imagines using his body as a human shield to save Marjorie, a non-combatant.

Finnegan drops the creature on the Vega Cacao tile in the kitchen, makes a peculiarly beautiful pepper-on-coffee swatch.

"Oh, Raymond. The poor thing."

In Raymond's hands, the animal's heart hums ever so faintly, like failing batteries in a plush toy. He says so and immediately regrets it.

"It's still *alive*? We can't let it suffer!"

Raymond is vaguely suspicious that *not letting it suffer* will come at some emotional cost for him, that the pronoun *we* has, long ago, been assigned a new number and a specific gender. Of course, that's what married couples do. Negotiating meaning is a silent auction. In their case, Marjorie orders take-out and presses the button on the robot vacuum. Raymond cleans the eavestroughs and murders living creatures.

But Marjorie tacks into the wind, exhales moral responsibility.

"Give it to me. I'll kill it."

"*What?* How?"

"I'll strangle it."

"Are you *kidding* me?"

"No, you just wring its neck. I saw my father do it to a chicken, once."

Raymond stares at Finnegan already on his back on the sofa, legs splayed and unmoving, his belly and genitals chapter and verse of a healthy body image. He can't help but make the connection between the hunter-swagger of that beast and his wife's inexplicable sang-froid.

"Marjorie, *no*." Raymond's go-to instinct is to protect his wife from anything and everything at all times. Still, he has to be careful. He can't *forbid* her to do anything, but he knows she would suffer terribly for her sacrifice. Emotional scars are his provide, his cross. She comes around to his way of thinking when he says, "You won't sleep."

"You're right, Raymond. I couldn't harm the bunny."

Suddenly, it's a *bunny* now that Raymond is its executioner. He thinks about asphyxiating the creature in a plastic produce bag from Walmart, but that seems prissy next to the hands-on mayhem suggested by his wife. He settles upon making a gallows noose of his thumb and forefinger. The pressure is everything. He is terrified of something unsavoury, like a death rattle or a decapitation.

Deed done, he retracts the compost bin from beneath the kitchen sink and drops the limp form of no-bunny-no-more on top of the coffee grounds and the remaining strands of last night's pad Thai. It is a distasteful thing to do. He feels faintly nauseous.

Marjorie pets Finny's ears, harvests emotional therapy that should be for him.

"Well," she says, "*we've* had a morning!"

"Yes," says Raymond, "*we* have."

*

That evening, he has already paid for parking at the airport when Marjorie suggests that *someone* return home and dispose of the rabbit.

"After a week, it'll really smell," she says. "We should have thought of that."

Of course, Marjorie is always right when it is least convenient. No one wants to return from a holiday in Spain to the smell of an abattoir. And Rachael, the neighbour, would feed and walk Finny, but they couldn't ask her to triage pad Thai and hare tartare. As a result, seeing Picasso's *Guernica* starts to feel less like a bucket list item and more like a labour of Hercules. "I'll take care of it," Raymond says, feigning free will.

Forty minutes later, he opens the compost bin and stares at the carcass with an escalating sense of dread and terror. The animal appears to have two things: an eyebrow of espresso grounds and no explanation for it. Unless, of course, it has somehow *turned its head*.

Raymond drops the lid on the compost bin. Had the rabbit still been alive? Had its dying gesture been one of mockery? *Raymond hath murdered sleep, and therefore Raymond shall sleep no more.* He thinks of Marjorie and the cords of wood she will saw beneath her smug duvet.

Okay, to exorcise the bloody deed, Raymond imagines running with the bulls in Pamplona, the vibration of hooves on the cobblestone a terror for terror gambit. In the meantime, he dons a pair of latex gloves, extracts the rabbit from its warren and gently places it inside a large format, freezer bag. In the basement, he parks the rabbit next to a bag of President's Choice frozen carrots. *Whose eyebrows are smiling now?*

Before leaving, Raymond showers Finny's lightly bearded muzzle with kisses. "Daddy doesn't blame you," he says. He is alone. He will risk it. "Daddy doesn't blame *you*."

*

At the airport, Raymond chugs toward customs with two pieces of carry-on luggage framing his imitation of a large-boned retiree with arthritic knees and elbows. If his arms and legs are no longer buds in the womb, it is because he has been crawling on all fours for too long. *Anyway*, thirty-seven years of exhausting chivalry preclude asking his wife to schlep her own personal effects. As a result, exertion produces bubbling resentment and patriarchy a reverse mortgage of their marriage. *See Raymond run,* he thinks, narrating from a Grade 3 Dick and Jane reader, *Streets and Roads, More Streets and Roads, Roads to Follow,* and *More Roads to Follow.*

Marjorie motions for Raymond to hurry. Marjorie mouths the words, *hurry, hurry, hurry!* Marjorie taps her wristwatch with her forefinger, one of two she might have used to execute the hare, if it hadn't been a bunny.

"Where have you *been*?" she says. "We're the last to board!"

Raymond stares crossly and toward the parallel security station. "The family" he says, grimly.

"What *family*?"

"Blood will have blood."

"You're scaring me, Raymond."

"The rabbits are circling the homestead."

Marjorie thinks that Raymond is teasing her, but her smile is the same she uses when Raymond jokes about his sexual needs. She won't encourage him.

Raymond reclaims his passport from the gate agents and turns to enter the boarding bridge to the airplane. Instead, moving his self-conflict in another direction, he looks behind himself to ensure Marjorie's safety and, if need be, to share a look of rebuke for his dawdling wife. If she wants to see that famous anti-war painting, she had best shake a leg.

But Marjorie is on a movie set of some sort, because she is receiving all kinds of direction and the same scenes require multiple takes. Twice, she passes through the metal detector and several times her carry-on bag is shunted backward and forward through the X-ray machine. Finally, a security officer unloads all the contents of her suitcase, unzips a side pocket and surfaces a wad of dog poop bags, remainders from the land trip to New York to procure Finnegan. The officer smells, pinches and scrutinizes the bags.

Marjorie looks flummoxed and imbecilic and terrified and Raymond blames himself for the misunderstanding. He should be with her to explain that she is a good person, that there is no reason to suspect her of anything other than that. And Marjorie would never transport contraband or weapons or explosives in her carry-on or in her body cavities. Almost to prove the point, she raises her arms like Christ on the cross and a security wand makes repeated snow angels of her innocence.

One of two gate agents says, "Sir, you have to board the airplane."

Raymond protests. "But my wife is still at customs!"

The second gate agent says, "You have to board, sir."

Raymond feels like a little boy from whom maternal care has been withdrawn, one who has to obey orders because terrified children will always do what they are told.

From his seat in the airplane and through the tiny window, he sees *disembodied Raymond* floating like a spacewalking astronaut whose tether has been cut. Because Marjorie will miss the flight, he has the irrational fear that he will never see her again or, worse, he *will* see her, a broken, abandoned version that trumps his own expanding universe of terror and loneliness. Why did he separate himself from Marjorie? Was he trying to punish her and for what possible reason?

But fear and self-loathing are a particle accelerator. Lickety-split, Raymond no longer feels like a young boy, but a very old man, as unlikely to protect Marjorie from the terror of airport security as he is to bathe and toilet himself. He looks toward the dark matter in the empty seat next to him. He can't see the dark matter but he can feel its gravitational effects in tumbling tears as hot as words: *Raymond, you are a failure as a husband. Raymond, codependency gives the lie to your hubris. What will you do, Raymond, now that fiction is a whale and you are spat or shat?*

Liftoff without Marjorie is a cocktail of anesthetics and methamphetamine. In hour five, the stewardess shepherds the beverage trolley beyond the red-eyed castaway in REM sleep.

He is running with the bulls in Pamplona except the bulls are not bulls but three-thousand-pound rabbits with espresso brows and swappable modular parts. Their size, number and momentum risk to crush him to bits. Naked Marjorie is there, too. From her hotel balcony, naked Marjorie can see Raymond's bald pate bobbing among undulating waves of saddle and shoulder. She tosses her carry-on baggage down to Raymond, bundle after bundle of personal effects that stick to Raymond as though his clothes were Velcro. Raymond screams above the din: for God's sake, Marjorie, they come on wheels now! You can pull your own damn shampoo! But these cubes of carry-on are not a burden, after all. They make of Raymond a multi-pillowed Transformer, an arthritis-free autobot impervious to the absurd power of the rabbit tide.

"Viva!" he mutters. "Gora!" Raymond's waking moment is infused with the brio of resistance. Now that Marjorie is a suspected terrorist, she needs him even more, needs Raymond to tilt his lance against the windmills of the security state.

He will return home immediately, because he knows what Marjorie will do, because he and she are from a time outside of time, one free of rabbits the size of bulls, personal baggage no longer your own and uniformed men and women who like to believe you are not human, except in your dreams.

Officers of Adaptation to Climate Change

Laura called me in Mozambique to say that mom had died. Our two-year vigil had ended. Anyway, could I be home in a week? We were all going to scatter her ashes at the cottage. In a subsequent text, she developed the plan. The ash scattering would coincide with the solar eclipse. *We've got a cosmic window to honor mom's memory.* Soon, another text arrived: *We'll stream the ceremony on Facebook Live.* Did I have a plane ticket, yet? Our younger sister, Becky, would also be there. *Love yuh, bro'.*

Laura was like that. Commemoration was a Christmas tree and a box of decorations. Life altering moments were hand-painted ornaments. Popular holidays were tinsel. And anniversaries were sepia strings of popcorn. Her industry was cheerful spin. In fact, she reminded me of an ice skater that has mastered perfectly closed circles. Anyway, I pushed back against Facebook Live. Minutes later, she sent a thumbs-up emoji.

Africa was only partially my idea. At the end of our last session, my psychiatrist suggested service to others as an antidote for loneliness. She probably meant the Daily Bread Food Bank or the Yonge Street Mission. I told her over the phone that I had chosen to volunteer for six weeks in Mozambique. I could tell she was surprised by the way she held her breath. "Travel far enough," she said, "to meet yourself."

I had been battling the beast of depression for twenty-five years. I had never married. I had no kids. I sometimes spent days in bed where my nearest companion was a urine collection container. Ironically, I was a successful headhunter for the arts and entertainment sector in Toronto. I could minister to the needs of any organization, but I couldn't help myself. In a lighter moment, before leaving for Mozambique, I hoped the beast didn't have a passport.

After one week of training, I earned my stripes as an officer of adaptation to climate change. I was working with young university grads who wore this new title easily, like an activity tracker. Anyway, it was our job to mentor people whose livelihoods had been destroyed by global warming. I saw what that looked like when we flew over the Larde district of Nampula province. A river with a thousand year history had vanished. All that remained was brown grass that looked like a parched earthworm.

A young woman named Carlina gave us the backstory: "There was too much sun. The river went away. The fish followed the river. Some tried to grow tobacco or cassava. Some collected bits of firewood to sell. The tobacco died. The cassava starved. The firewood followed the fish into memory."

Carlina's eyes and voice communicated a deep well of sadness. Instinctively, I drank and thirsted for more. She was a twenty-one-year-old divorcee (barren, I was told) who lived with her parents. Six years earlier, she had been a child bride given by her father to a man more than twice her age. *The river left. The fish left. There were many mouths to feed.* My thoughts about Carlina came immediately and fully formed. I wondered if her father might - yet again - bless her union with a man twice her age. My psychiatrist's words were all the rationale I needed. I had travelled far enough to meet myself. Would I be able to love myself?

Courtship of Carlina reminded me of my very first courtship. I would go to dances in middle school and lean against a wall in the gymnasium. A girl I liked did exactly the same. Through the darkness, we would look at each other furtively, the first time and all other times. At evening's end, we would embrace and move slowly to Led Zeppelin's "Stairway to Heaven".

Carlina and I watched each other like that, secretly and through the darkness in our hearts, until she took my hand and said, "Come see." I thought about Led Zeppelin, the zeppelin called the Hindenburg, the fire that destroyed it and the stairway to heaven. I was all in from the get-go.

The return trip to Canada gave me a glimpse of what life would be like. Carlina travelled in traditional dress, bold yellow and pink colours and a sweeping bolt of cloth around her body and over one shoulder. I was no longer a wallflower. I was the greying white guy travelling with a young and dazzling black woman. I imagined people's thoughts like falling ticker at a parade: I was a predator or a colonizer or a marriage tourist of spent virtue.

Of course, I repurposed these thought bubbles into trial balloons that put me in the best possible light. I told myself that I was no more sexist or racist than those who might judge me. Was my new wife a victim simply because she was an African and a woman? That kind of thinking was automatic writing from an old culture. I shared these thoughts with Carlina, worried about my own posturing. She said, "You have seen my lupembe?" I had seen her *lupembe*. It was a wind instrument made of animal horn. "Each is handmade and unique. It can be no other way." I wrapped my arm around hers. I felt unbelievably happy.

Everyone met us at the airport in Winnipeg. I had texted Laura about Carlina. I knew she would bring the others up to speed. Our plan was to drive straightway to the cottage. Becky gave me the kind of hug that comes with a deployed airbag. I knew she was there under duress. Laura said that the urn containing mom's ashes was in a cup holder in the car, right next to the coffee from Starbucks. "If we're not careful," she said, "we'll eulogize Blond Vanilla Latte." Anyway, we had two hours of road before us and a *cosmic window*. She hugged me and whispered in my ear, "You could be her father." It was easy cruelty, because it was true.

But it was dad that I had seen first. I looked at him through the window on the customs side of arrivals. He was coyote thin. His right arm rested on a portable oxygen machine. Of late, his speech was unfiltered and impulsive, bytes of memory, observation and occasional obscenity. Dementia was giving him a scrabble board and few vowels to play with. Anyway, it was a miracle that mom had lived into her eighties and that dad was still alive. Both had smoked cigarettes since their mid-teens, become fierce enablers of one another.

In fact, I'm still haunted by memories of their toxic routine. In the living room, they had easy chairs, ashtrays, books and a carton of cigarettes. They read, smoked and cleared their throats through days and years. I and Laura and Becky went our separate ways into the basement or into our rooms. We were environmental refugees and asylum seekers. Through time, we convinced ourselves that family was damage and isolation. My psychiatrist clarified one point for me: "If you and your sisters felt unloved, I'm guessing your parents didn't need cigarettes to do that."

In the car, Carlina was in the back seat next to Becky who was next to my dad. I was beside Laura up front. I had a pretty good idea what Becky was saying to Carlina. She was a wounded soul and a broken record. Anyway, it didn't occur to me to ask about Laura's husband until we were in the car.

"Where's Mitch?"

Laura said, "I have no idea. We're not married, anymore."

I was stunned. I asked her what happened.

"Life happened."

I had taken little or no interest in Laura and Mitch. She owed me nothing in the way of explanation.

"What about the kids?"

"The kids are with me. We all celebrate holidays together."

I noticed that Laura was checking her speed and her mirrors constantly. She wanted me to know that she was managing everything just fine. "Jesus," I said, "I'm really sorry."

Laura's eyes stayed on the speedometer, the mirrors and the road. "Couples have been falling apart since forever. You know what mom used to say - *Don't cry in your pork chops*."

In spite of myself, I pushed forward in a small voice, "Why didn't you tell me?"

Laura stiffened and threw a fastball. "Mitch and I both make good money, Steve. You couldn't have saved us." It was easy cruelty, because it was true. Carlina had nothing. I had money and the unspoken belief that I could use it to trade for anything. I didn't know how to think about my privilege or to what degree I had simply monetized my needs. I was the best and the worst of myself all at once.

Anyway, Laura, the ice skater, looked at me directly and produced another perfectly closed circle, "Hashtag failure, bro'. It's over."

I knew we would never talk about this, again. *It's over* was her one and only post.

While we sat in silence, dad snored, Becky talked and Carlina listened. Intermittently, I turned down the air conditioner. I was trying to hear what was going on in the back seat. Laura noticed my fiddling and commented, "What's up with you and the AC?" I answered truthfully and evasively, "I'm an officer of adaptation to climate change."

True to form, Becky was introducing herself by way of a familiar theme. She left home when she was still a teenager. She quit school and moved in with her girlfriend. After twenty years of conjugal bliss, Renée, her girlfriend, moved out and shacked up with some low-life guy. "I gave her the best years of my life and she shit on me." Becky could be vulgar and completely unselfconscious. She described to Carlina examples of *kinko sex* demanded by her ex.

When I was a kid, I resented Becky. It had nothing to do with age or gender or property. I resented her because she had managed early release from our failed home. In adulthood, my attitude toward her was more conflicted. On the one hand, it couldn't have been easy for her to live as an openly gay person. She was the first heroine I knew who didn't come from the pages of books at school. On the other hand, after her split with Renée, she wore emotional pain like cosmetic scars. These were ugly and she chose ugly language to describe them. It was hard to testify to anything that might derail her own self-absorption.

Or so I thought. I heard Carlina say to Becky, "They cut my genitals when I was four. I cannot have children. My first husband took me sexually when I was still a girl. I sometimes pee where and when I shouldn't. It was my job to get water from the well. Village boys knew this was my job. It was a long walk and they knew. You and I are sisters."

I put on my sunglasses and started to cry. Carlina added something else I couldn't hear and Becky fell silent for the remainder of the trip.

When we got to the cottage, Laura said we had precious little time to get into the water. The solar eclipse would start in minutes. I helped dad out of the car and steered him toward the lake. Carlina walked beside me, too. She had her small travel bag in one hand.

At the dock, I sat dad down and removed his shoes and socks. I said to my dad, "We're going to put mom's ashes in the water. She loved it here. Do you remember?"

My dad said, "Oh, yeah, sure."

Of course, my own memories were less burnished. Mom and dad used to recline in chairs on the dock and smoke and read. As small children, I and my sisters would swim and compete for their attention until, of course, we stopped.

And then dad said something that horrified me. He had forgotten his introduction to Carlina. With her at my side, he said, "Is this your darkie?"

I hadn't heard that awful word in decades and the idea of possession almost made me scream. Like others from their generation, mom and dad were casual racists. In this case, dreadful habits were a feedback loop. They would sometimes share offensive language and opinions while darkening their own lungs with tar. Anyway, I looked at this sick, old man and measured my response. And then I listened to Carlina's answer. She repeated herself word for word from the airport lobby, "I am from Africa. I am your son's wife. My name is Carlina. It is good to meet you."

We were up to our knees in lake water, mostly hand in hand in a small circle. If I felt degrees of separation from my parents and my sisters, wearing solar eclipse glasses did not help. We looked like witnesses to a nuclear bomb test. Not far from the truth, really. Nor did it help that the sky was darkening and midday became twilight. Laura's cosmic window was a funeral home with drawn curtains. Suddenly, I regretted my veto of Facebook Live. Performing for a camera might have given us our best chance for closure.

No one spoke. We were supposed to take turns honoring mom's memory, but no one said a word. Becky had already refused to take anybody's hand. Laura couldn't find the strength to decorate the tree. And Dad did his part, too. A cigarette hung from his lips as he stared at the waning sun. As for me, I was filled with guilt and resistance, hope from an ocean away and despair up to my knees. We couldn't manage a good life together and, it seemed, we couldn't manage a good death, either. We were utterly and impossibly dysfunctional.

That's when Carlina rested her travel bag in my arm and proceeded to extract her lupembe. I had never heard her play before. The sound was mellow and warm and heraldic. It gave dignity to my family that I didn't believe possible. Laura moved to the last part of the ceremony and shook out mom's ashes into the lake water. For the first time, God help me, I felt compassion for my father. He and my mom had always been the sum of one and one and less than more. How did he feel seeing her atomized remains returned to the DNA of the world? We all cried and I suspect for different reasons.

Anyway, after Carlina finished her song and while the sun hid behind the moon, she whispered in my ear, "I am become an officer of adaptation to climate change." I wanted to give her my very best hug, but I had her own travel bag under one arm and dad's oxygen machine under the other. I leaned forward to kiss her and say, "You won't have to carry the water alone."

Gods, Titans and Junk

The penis was huge and erect. The testicles were proportional and egg-shaped. It would be fair to say that most of Marlene's observable world was a giant blue penis and giant blue testes. It was like standing at the base of a missile with a warhead. Of course, this perspective wasn't unique to her experience. Having jumbo male genitalia in the crosshairs was always a data dump seeking an interpreter.

Anyway, Rajeev had invited his wife to come see a spectacular penis, something he routinely assigned a third person pronoun and a masculine gender. Marlene was both incredulous and annoyed. She had seen this pop-up book before. Rajeev seemed not to understand that *spectacular penis* could be an oxymoron, that fireworks require oxygen or things like conversation and consent.

But Rajeev was in his surrealist period. He now believed in ignored associations and creative acts of revolt; in other words, every nook and cranny in the house was fresh opportunity for penetration. As a result, Marlene exited the bathroom that morning with a mental note: what room or appliance had not already provided uncomfortable angles and post-coital bruises?

As it happens, the penis was not Rajeev's. Marlene came to the window in the living room and followed the line of sight from Rajeev's finger. Much of the sky was filled with a giant blue penis and a giant blue scrotum, the outline of which appearing to be the product of jet exhaust. Rajeev said as much, "Someone in an airplane has done this. Can you believe it?"

Marlene returned her gaze to the giant blue penis and the giant blue scrotum. The glans of the penis pointed upward and in the direction of a white cumulus cloud that looked like a discharge of semen. Marlene didn't know if the composition was premeditated or accidental. And she didn't know how she felt about what she was seeing. In any event, the image was already losing its integrity, like a Snapchat photo.

Rajeev attracted his wife's attention. "Marlene," he said, smiling and tapping the pane of glass, "this is called a single hung window." Her husband laughed, but she didn't understand the joke at all. Sometimes, they seemed not to speak the same language.

*

Home from university for the weekend, Swati embraced her parents and said, "Did you guys see that huge cock in the sky?"

Shouted Marlene, "Swati! My God!" Neither Marlene nor Rajeev would reprimand Swati. University had empowered her with remarkable ideas and the conviction to speak plainly.

Swati developed her text as she slipped off her camouflage field jacket: "A pilot in the air force did it. It's condensation. It's called a contrail. Conspiracy theorists call it a chemtrail, a toxic mist that poisons everything we do. But it's not! A chemtrail is a con job. Is that confusing, mother?"

Swati was wearing a multifunctional, unisex garment consisting of tank top, dress, cape and wings. The color palette was mostly nude and black. Marlene looked at her daughter's outfit and said without enthusiasm, "This is nice." She never knew what words to choose, if compliments or observations of any sort were appropriate.

Said Swati, "That pilot should get the Gaia treatment."

Rajeev didn't know what *Gaia treatment* meant, but it sounded menacing. He excused himself to go to work. He drove a bus for the Municipal Authority.

Swati called after him, "Wait! I have to ask you questions about your sex life!"

Marlene prepared dandelion tea, while Swati gave her the dope about Gaia. "Mother Earth was pissed off with Uranus humping her 24/7, so she persuaded her son, Cronus, to chop off his dad's junk. Get this, mom. He used a sickle or *bagging hook,* the same tool for harvesting or *raping*. Really and truly divine retribution. Let the punishment fit the crime!"

Marlene said she favored progressive discipline. "Couldn't they give the pilot a fine or community service?"

Swati protested. "What? Are you kidding me? This is bigger than a Mount Rushmore prick. This is about misogyny and paternalism. Men think they own the world! Imagine how entitled you must feel to paint the horizon with a huge blood sausage." Swati paused to amplify her summation. "That penis was a giant middle finger directed at a woman's vagina."

Marlene wanted to segue into another topic. Regrettably, Swati had already loaded onto her computer the survey for her Human

Sexuality class. The questions were intimate and invasive. Marlene only heard key words and phrases through the fog of war: *how many fingers… kinds of toys… role-play… porn preferences.* It did not help that her daughter read these questions with clinical detachment.

With each answer of *no* or *not applicable*, Marlene felt more humiliated. She wanted to tell her daughter that she and Swati's father had made love in the heron position and in the praying mantis position, that her parents had turned every room in the house into a carnal fitness centre and that, in fact, Swati's kitchen chair had been towelled off more than once. But this would be embarrassing. Instead, Marlene blurted out, "Anything goes, except pain! I don't like pain!" Marlene didn't know why she had lied, why her response wasn't entirely truthful.

Swati tabulated the results of her sex test and sighed. The demographic represented by her parents produced a line of data virtually identical to the horizontal axis. She sipped tea and tacked in a different direction. "Mother, we're going to talk about zie, zim, zir, zis and zieself."

Marlene's face was like that of a sphinx.

"These are gender inclusive pronouns. We must no longer use language to pass judgement. Too many people live with chronic unease and dissatisfaction. It's called *dysphoria.* Don't worry," Swati said. "We'll practice during the weekend. It's not like the old pronouns are genetic code. Are you listening, mother?"

*

Rajeev often joked that Marlene was more his teacher than his wife. Because she taught art history courses at the college, she slipped easily into Socratic mode.

Later that day, he had barely closed the front door behind him when Marlene thrust her iPad into his face. She had been researching Swati's reference to mythical gods, titans and junk.

"The painting is called, *Castration of Uranus.*" The title was misleading since the aftermath was the subject. Indeed, Cronus was absconding with the severed penis of his father. The penis was as long as a femur and as wide as a thigh.

"Here's where things get interesting."

Rajeev listened, but he appeared forlorn.

"Look at the three principal figures."

Mechanically, Rajeev looked at Cronus and Gaia and Uranus. His gaze rested on the huge severed penis. Marlene did not notice right away, but Rajeev's eyes were moist.

"None of them looks sad or surprised or horrified or anything. It's like Christ going to the cross."

Rajeev didn't know what that meant.

Marlene added, "It *had* to happen. Don't you see? It *has* to happen!"

"Darling," said Rajeev, touching her wrist. "I have testicular cancer."

Marlene's mouth opened and the hand holding the tablet floated to her side. Rajeev did not go to work today. Rajeev had a follow-up appointment to see his doctor. Marlene had forgotten these things because Rajeev swam laps in the pool every morning. The cremaster muscle was to blame. His wandering testicle and tender groin were the result of contracting muscles in the cold water. The follow-up appointment was a formality intended to confirm their own online diagnosis.

"Oh, Rajeev."

They held each other for almost exactly two minutes. In fact, Rajeev compared this period of consolation to the ceremony of remembrance at the Delhi War Cemetery, not the *silence*, itself, but the bugle call that traditionally follows it. "Marlene," he said, "your comfort is like the *Last Post* for the penis of Rajeev."

To prove the point, Rajeev surfaced pamphlets from his pockets and began reading. Marlene felt like she was suspended alive in a syrupy cryonic solution. Key words and phrases were opaque bubbles: *removal of the testicle... insertion of a prosthetic, saline-filled testicle... radiation therapy... lymph nodes.* Rajeev was overcome with emotion when he recited statistics concerning erectile dysfunction. Marlene made matters worse when she said intercourse didn't matter to her. Rajeev understood it to mean denial of his personhood or, worse, criticism of his sexual performance.

"Anyway," he said, "well - ." He informed Marlene that he would prefer that their daughter not know. He had his own reasons. Marlene protested, but Rajeev insisted. "No," he said. "I forbid it! Do as I say!" Only then did Marlene cry at her husband's news.

Swati arrived at the mention of her name. In the hallway, she heard her father bark commands.

"I'm sorry, dad," she said, "but you don't get to talk to mom like that."

Marlene and Rajeev looked like Easter Island statues, inscrutable to themselves.

Swati said that Rajeev should examine the socio-cultural reasons for his browbeating of her mother.

Marlene wiped her nose on her sleeve and said, "Not now, Swati. You don't know what you're talking about."

Swati said she knew *exactly* what she was talking about. She explained the intersectionality of oppression, how things like sexism, classism and racism collectively persecute women.

Marlene's face expanded like a blowfish. "Are you *insane*? Your father is an Indian! He drives a bus!" She immediately regretted her defence of Rajeev.

Swati rebutted, "The penis trumps everything!"

Marlene thought she might be able to reason her way out of this painful misunderstanding, but she lacked the energy and the will. Instead, she said, "Shut up, Swati! That's it! Do you hear?"

Swati returned to her room. She did not begrudge her mother. Victims often play foolish enablers to their victimizers. It was a cultural inheritance.

Rajeev took the iPad from Marlene's hand and pointed at the huge, severed penis of Uranus. "Gaia had Cronus. You have Swati. Perhaps," he added, "I will drive a bus more comfortably."

They embraced once again.

*

Until then, Marlene had always resisted *that*. Rajeev would drop hints from time to time, like letters meant for her, but not from him. Or he would linger in that particular erogenous zone, make contact *accidentally* and camouflage his wilfulness with a berserk sex drive. Marlene was not unsophisticated. She knew what was going on.

But the cancer diagnosis produced urgency for each of them. Rajeev was convinced that he would become impotent soon with "so much", he said, "left undone." Marlene had read the same pamphlet. She was skeptical. Nonetheless, she knew that her husband's hysteria was perfectly credible.

For this reason, and kindness and charity, she went to a sex shop and bought a lubricant called Eros. She informed Rajeev that she was open to *that* while the sail was full and the wind strong. He looked at her as a man who has won temporary reprieve from a horrible death.

The supper meal produced conversation and lasagna that were largely ignored. After Rajeev brought Green Dragon tea to his bedroom, Swati spread her school books over the table as Marlene stacked dishes in the dishwasher.

Swati thought that whatever she said would antagonize her mother. For this reason, she would not respect any filter, at all. "And you know what he did with his father's schlong?"

Marlene sighed heavily as she pulled out the top drawer of the dishwasher. "Again with Cronus? God help me, how much penis can I take?"

"He tossed the whole package into the sea. And from the bloody foam emerged Aphrodite, the maiden goddess of pleasure and procreation. Sometimes, mother, and this is where it gets interesting, Aphrodite was portrayed armed and bearded."

Marlene continued to load dishes. She did not look at her daughter. "So, according to you, I should stop waxing and buy a weapon?"

"You're stronger than you think, mother."

Marlene wanted to say, *and you're not as smart as you think.* Instead, she looked at dinner plates in the top rack of the dishwasher, teacups sitting in cutlery compartments and a tablet of dishwasher cleaner where detergent should be. She took her face into her hands and wept quietly.

Swati was quickly at Marlene's side. "Don't worry," she said, catching her mother's tears on her shoulder. "We can fix this. You may be my mom, but we're sisters, too."

*

Later that night, Rajeev lit beeswax candles and plugged in the fragrance diffuser. He turned on the television and amplified music from the spa channel. None of this seemed ludicrous to Rajeev. Sometimes, exchanges are imperfect. Love and faith restore balance. The bottle of Eros at his bedside was merely one bead on an abacus.

Marlene entered the bedroom in her paisley nightgown. She climbed into the bed and rolled onto her side, her back facing Rajeev.

After a few seconds, she hiked up her gown to expose her buttocks. After a few more seconds, Rajeev straddled the bed on his knees. The angle and gravity created by his weight were like a tide pulling her in.

Rajeev finished undressing Marlene and began to squeeze and pinch where the flesh was greatest. Next, he used his fingers to investigate the contours and creases of her body. In either instance, he often used the ruse of misjudgement, the game he played expanding boundaries imagined and self-imposed. All the while, Marlene inhaled Temple Smoke, beard oil that smelled of oakmoss and sandalwood.

Afterward, the kisses that found her neck, back and bottom were not unpleasant. Marlene tried to focus on these things because her own fear was setting selfish ideas against her resolve. It helped when Rajeev whispered his great love. She turned just enough to say the same but, equally, to confirm his erection.

Next, Rajeev squirted lubricant into one hand. The bottle made a farting sound. Rajeev said, "Sorry." He worried that the farting sound would sabotage the romance of candles, diffuser and music. Marlene seemed indifferent to the farting sound.

While Rajeev positioned her legs and applied dollops of Eros, Marlene's clenched jaw concealed intractable questions. Had not Gaia, also the goddess of prophecy, foreseen millions or billions of years of rape and dysphoria? Why did their daughter judge her father abominable and her mother impotent? Had Cronus been moved by ambition or mercy? And what, exactly, *has* to happen, if anything at all?

Marlene could not say if her screams were involuntary or premeditated, if she cried out for pain or absolution or recognition.

But it was no surprise when she heard Swati pound at the bedroom door. And it was no surprise when she heard inclusive pronouns accuse someone or persons of gross misconduct. And it was no surprise that these things were wholly parenthetical to the snorting sobs of her husband and how he cried for sorrow and regret.

In fact, reflexively, Marlene had already repurposed her own tears to shelter the blue chemtrail penis that continued to pump her anus.

Empire in the Gardens of Babylon

Fatima recognized one of the human heads. She said to her brother, "This particular head belonged to the fighter, Michael." Michael was an Englishman who joined the Sons of Ahwah. Everyone knew Michael. There was a swath of Sheffield in the uncovered space around his eyes, like a racoon. Michael displeased the Sons of Ahwah because he wore Union Jack boxers beneath his uniform.

Being clever, Fatima easily updated her biographical understanding of all things. "*Saint Michael*," she said, "is the one who raped Mahdia."

"Don't talk stupid," Umar said. "He fixed the internet."

Fatima was undeterred. "You can fix the internet *and* rape Mahdia."

"You're a pig," Umar said. "How do you know these things? *How*?"

Fatima said that women and girls share a kind of *sad commerce*. They barter news of the abominations of men and no one is any wiser or richer for the knowledge.

Umar counterpointed by saying that he, too, was sad. The plan was to use the heads as goalposts in the abandoned car park. But none of his friends came to play football. He had worn his *Lions of Mesopotamia* jersey for absolutely nothing.

Umar gathered up the heads into a burlap sack and slung it over his shoulder. He took Fatima's hand, which he always did, even if she had the heart of an executioner. His father once said to him, prophetically, as it turned out, "If I am not here, you must take care of the girls and your mother." Umar imagined easier work wearing a suicide vest.

It was bad luck that the interior of the marble factory had been blown out by allied bombs and that the hole in one wall made a direct line of sight through the window frame in another wall. Three Sons of Ahwah fighters spotted two of the six heads floating above the shards of marble mortuary. The Sons of Ahwah fighters were all dressed in black, like cowboys from an old American Western whose clothing, alone, telegraphed their intentions.

Fatima and Umar froze in their steps, like statues of the dictator before the liberation of his people.

One of the Sons of Ahwah fighters took the bag from Umar and struck him forcefully in the face with the palm of his hand. The others trained their rifles upon the boy. Apparently, the girl was useless. The contents of the bag were emptied onto the ground.

Fatima was a callous documentarian of human behaviour and, as a result, clever as a fox. She needed a *coup* of some sort that would be a talisman against her brother's beating and her own possible lashing or rape. A curfew was a curfew. Examples must be made.

Fatima gathered the heads of the Sons of Ahwah traitors into a tight square. She squatted over the heads of the Sons of Ahwah traitors, lifted her skirt and produced a stream of urine and demonic curses. Subsequently, she grunted and exposed her horse's teeth while defecating a mealy rope of half-digested rice, saffron and mint.

The three Sons of Ahwah fighters managed disgust in three different languages, but they all wore the same choral mask from Greek tragedy. No one was fooling anyone.

After the fighters had left, Umar said to his sister, "You're a pig." He added, "And you've ruined my goalposts."

Fatima did not have a reply for that. Football was serious business.

When they got home, they could hear their little sister mimicking their mother. "IN-DI-A-NA" she would say or "O-HI-O." Home schooling was the thing since the Sons of Ahwah came to town. For some few weeks, Anaam had sent Shaimaa to one of the Sons of Ahwah schools, but the idiot child (so called by her mother) was not a discerning pupil in any respect. Her homework would include repeatedly drawing and coloring the Sons of Ahwah flag. Her mother would not tolerate it.

Anaam interrupted her lesson between California and Minnesota. These days, she always looked at her children with a mixture of contempt and pity. One fueled the other and created a kind of septic anger, shit always at the ready to hit the fan. "It's dark! Where have you been?"

Because Fatima had already told him what to say, Umar spoke with charm and authority.

"It is like this, dear mother."

He said his sister had to use the public toilet, which was true enough, because their toilet had been smashed to bits by Sons of

Ahwah fighters looking for contraband. And it was also true that Umar always accompanied the females out of doors. It was one of the *Laws of the Sons of Ahwah*. Umar did not mention shameful acts that would surely offend Allah.

Once again, Anaam recognized arrogance in her son's tone. Obviously, his sister's lies would embolden him, but there was more to it than that. Umar was making a seamless transition toward scorn for women simply because he was empowered to do so.

For this reason, Anaam aspirated profanity behind her veil. Umar's ears pricked immediately, like those of a dog. He discerned possibly unpleasant syllables in his mother's whispered, humid dispatches. Anyway, the *niqab* was a great diplomat.

Anaam said to Umar, "Swear on your father's beard!" And she produced a potpourri bag full of her husband's *lihyah*. She kept the beard hair in an interior pocket of her cloak.

Because Omar, their father, had lived on principle, he did not live long. He was a barber when the Sons of Ahwah usurped control of the city. He refused to believe that growing the beard was *wajib* or mandatory and, after weeks of grudging conformity, shaved, with an electric razor, no less, to protest beard fetishism.

Unfortunately, Omar underestimated the threat of the Sons of Ahwah, calling them *a few bad apples* and *a little boys club*. He took his naked face outside and was never seen again, become, as Fatima liked to say, wistfully, one of the supernatural beings or *jinn*. To which, her mother said, "Have you no feelings?" Fatima said that if feelings could be attached to kebab, she would welcome them instantly.

Umar touched the bristling remains of his father's beard and produced a peculiar spectacle. He declined his head and raised his hand, as if his testimony were legal and incontrovertible. "I swear," he said, "to nothing but the truth."

At the same time that Anaam screamed, "Liar!", Fatima broke her silence with an angry announcement of her own. "We need *meat*, mother! I have more diarrhea than the prime minister!"

Anaam wanted to slap Umar and Fatima. It was just a matter of deciding whose insolence deserved the quicker rebuke. Instead, she settled upon gallows humour, literally. "You want meat?" she asked. "Then, go to the butcher shop!"

The *butcher shop* was the town square where criminals were hung or decapitated by the Sons of Ahwah for crimes great and small. Umar had collected his goalposts there.

Fatima wanted to say that she was, at least, open to the *idea* of cannibalism. After all, animal protein had largely disappeared at about the same time as local *imams* were replaced by vegetarians from neighbouring states or so cause and effect would have it.

But her mother raised her hand in the air to signal the limit of her endurance. "Whatever you say," she said, looking wearily at Fatima, "it will mean my death. Go to bed. All of you. It exhausts me being your mother." *Going to bed* meant carving out space on a shared mattress beneath one comforter whose theme was Mickey Mouse and his Magic Kingdom. All other mattresses and linen were *donated* to the hospital for the Sons of Ahwah fighters.

The next day began with mixed media – the cry of a child, the hum of unmanned, aerial vehicles and a clear blue sky. The idiot child (so called by her mother) opened her eyes at the same time as the *muezzin* began his pre-dawn call to prayer. Shortly thereafter, at daybreak, Shaimaa immediately started screaming, "Virginia! Nevada!"

Fatima owed a deep debt of gratitude to one of the heads that she had recently pissed and shat upon. Because *Saint Michael* had fixed the internet, she learned that drones were often controlled in Virginia and Nevada. As a result, she taught her sister to scream the names of these states whenever the day broke blue. Clear skies meant American drones would buzz the city looking for targets for their missiles.

As a result, it was important to avoid those places on drone days where the Sons of Ahwah fighters might gather – hospitals, schools, mosques, industries, private homes and markets. Of course, the fear of being atomized instantly was an existential threat and, therefore, somewhat less worrisome than lifestyle modifications such as lashing or amputation.

Anyway, Anaam knew what everyone was thinking and announced, "I'm going to the market. I don't care. Allah is good because his servants can only die once." And she immediately donned her burqa and began stuffing the interior pockets with beauty products. Before the re-introduction of the seventh century, Anaam worked with her husband, not as a barber, but as a beautician. Like a dragon, she stored her remaining hoard in the root cellar beneath the mattress. It was better than currency.

Several of the crowd at the market had *some* money with which to purchase onions, potatoes, garlic and the occasional orange or lemon. Most of the crowd had little or no money and, like Anaam, arrived at the market with goods to barter. Because the women were dressed in black and because their movement winnowed like a giant cloud of sand, they called their furtive trade a *black market haboob*.

Ahmed, a vegetable salesman, quickly assessed the eyes and height of Anaam, "I know you. You're like the others who look but don't buy. Move away and let pass women with money."

Anaam said she was interested in what *couldn't* be seen. She gestured with her head toward the Coca Cola cooler. Legend had it that the cooler contained skewers of marinating lamb.

"Even if you could see it," said Ahmed, "you couldn't buy it. Get away!"

Anaam retorted, "I cannot see Allah, but I love him deeply!" It was blasphemy to compare Allah to lamb kebabs but these were difficult times.

Of course, Ahmed was right. The women continued to circulate like rabid brokers at the stock exchange, but few were buying from the merchants. Their numbers far exceeded actual market capitalization. It was all very suspicious.

As for Anaam, locomotion was difficult. Within multiple pockets sewn into the lining of her burqa were many clear glass, round bottles with black pumps, representatives of Maybelline, L'Oréal, Clinique and Estee Lauder, among others. As a result, her thighs and buttocks were often bruised by trundling about like a heavily laden camel. Fortunately, this time, there would be no wasted movement. Her rich friend, Rahma, was the size of an aircraft carrier in the Persian Gulf.

Anaam whispered into Rahma's ear, "I have the avocado mask and the Dead Sea mud and," for somewhat comic effect, "all the perfumes of Arabia." She identified the prices and Rahma was only too happy to place her order and pay. *How vain you must be!* thought Anaam, since all women were compelled to cover their faces and wear gloves.

But Anaam did not know that she, too, was judged harshly, that others believed she did the devil's work, bartering lotions and creams that whispered into the hearts of her helpless victims. Because of Anaam, children swallowed soupy confections of rice and onions while their mothers applied candlelit complexions.

Of course, it would be risky to purchase the lamb skewers. A sudden windfall would draw attention from the vendors and the Sons of Ahwah minders. Nonetheless, and before the four of them were extinct, she wanted to provide one last serving of meat to her misogynist son, her glib, sociopathic daughter, and her last idiot child (so called by her mother).

She had only just purchased and hidden her precious cargo when all hell broke loose. Rahma had dropped a fragrance bomb and followed the bottle to the ground, casting about like a deranged shepherd for her lost sheep. Regrettably, reunion with her *Bois Noir*, (*for men*, no less), clinched the prosecution's case. Sons of Ahwah fighters circled, their vintage Kalashnikovs at the ready.

Immediately, Rahma's clothing was torn and stripped from her body, both her burqa and her undergarment of embroidered tulip on black. From various pockets, crevices and folds fell chocolates, olives, camembert, a Swiss army knife and kerosene. While she wept and screamed, Rahma was slapped, kicked, punched and called disgusting names. Finally, by her long, black hair with caramel highlights, two Sons of Ahwah soldiers pulled her through the dust and toward the interrogation centre.

At some distance away, moving very quickly and attaching her eyes to the ground, Anaam was breathless with both horror and elation. Already, imagination had produced a dog's muzzle of her nose, filled either nostril with the smell of roasting lamb and the flayed flesh of Rahma. She calmed her conscience with the assurance that everyone would end up dead or tortured eventually and, therefore, in such an environment, the procurement of lamb kebabs did not come with moral baggage.

Later that night, after the great debauch of kebab and fried aubergine, Fatima suggested that they offer a prayer for Rahma.

Anaam was caught off guard and assumed a defensive posture, "What do you mean by that?"

Fatima shrugged her shoulders and spoke calmly, as though she were merely underscoring the contribution of a corporate sponsor: "As you have stated, mother, the evening meal was brought to us by Rahma."

Anaam had avoided description of the unpleasant scene at the market. Rahma's hubris had cost her dearly. The children were apprised of the first instance, not the second. As a result, she assumed, the lamb had no bitter aftertaste.

However, and before Anaam could offer praise to Allah for the commerce of Rahma, Fatima insinuated her demonic eyes and horse's teeth not three inches from her mother's face. "Yes," she said, "let us offer a prayer of *long life* for Rahma." One did not need to study the Koran to read Fatima's sarcasm and the reason for it. News travels fast.

It was a painful barb. Anaam had assumed that constant supervision of her children would produce something like the Stockholm syndrome, uncritical love of their captor. But the opposite was true. For serving lamb, she was a scapegoat for the sins of the Sons of Ahwah.

Said Umar, in the somewhat twisted logic of his addled brain, "It is like this, dear mother. One day you are here and the next, you can't organize a football game."

Anaam became enraged. "Get into the other room!" she screamed. "All of you! And bring the mattress!" She thrust the idiot child (so called by her mother) into Fatima's arms and intoned gravely, "You can all sleep in there tonight."

But Umar, dragging the mattress with little enthusiasm and contemplating resistance, said the following, "Who are *you* to order *me*?"

Anaam knew immediately that this was the last order he would take from her. "I am your mother." The card was played. There were no more. Umar and the others retreated into the spare room.

After she had closed the door on her tormentors, Anaam curled into a fetal position on the Micky Mouse comforter. She might have cried for the loss of her husband, the loss of her friend or even the loss of her own estranged children, but, instead, she cried for fear, fear that Rahma, a kind of Freemason in a maternal order of secrets, would provide all the testimony necessary to have Anaam tortured or hung. In fact, she could not have imagined the quality of her divination nor the remarkable prescience of its messenger.

Indeed, she and her grown children were woken at three in the morning by Shaimaa, the *messenger*. Perhaps the idiot child (so called by her mother) was an idiot savant, after all. She began screaming "Texas! Texas! Texas!"

Because *Saint Michael* had fixed the internet, Fatima had read about *forced entry* in the Longhorn state, taught Shaimaa to scream *Texas* at the first sign of law enforcement. It was the work of an angel or a devil that Shaimaa began screaming well before the arrival of Sons of Ahwah fighters.

Fatima poked her weary head out of the spare room, said, "Listen, mother. This is bad news for you."

But it was also bad news for Umar. Not only did the Sons of Ahwah fighters arrest Anaam, but they conscripted the boy, too. Afterward, Fatima looked at Shaimaa on her back in the Mickey Mouse linen, said, "A useless warning is a house on fire." It did not occur to her to blame the child's teacher. It *did* occur to her that she, of the whole cursed family, had received the cruelest blow, left to care for another human being.

The very next day, the *bad apples* and *little boys* on the Sons of Ahwah Board of Authority published their decision. Anaam and Rahma were to be thrown off the roof of the tallest building in town, a radio station. Fatima read the details of the *fatwah* attached to a traffic sign that enjoined against noise, *No Horning*. She was stunned.

Apparently, Anaam was not being punished for her crimes against the seventh century, but her crimes against the twenty-first century. It was news to Fatima that her mother, *the capitalist whore*, had committed massive fraud before the arrival of the Sons of Ahwah, filling the very best brand name packaging with generic product. Fatima tried to imagine how much or how little suffering her mother had endured. She liked to think that Anaam spoke swiftly, not to avoid blood-letting, but to make herself right with Allah before she was executed.

Fatima's little sister was glued to her left leg. She detached the idiot child (so called by her mother) and shared an observation both sanguine and philosophical: "It is a world without moral center when perpetrators of legitimate criminal activity receive the same punishment as those addicted to cigarettes or hubble-bubble." It was unclear from her tone which group she reproved.

Shaimaa was ambivalent. "Washington" she said.

That night, Fatima's subconscious gerrymandered fresh boundaries for her dreams. Her mother was tossed from the roof of the radio station, but, miraculously, she planed through the air like a flying squirrel, lift provided by the ample folds within the inseam of her burqa. She flew to the capital and to all the great capitals of all the great states and then into outer space and through the Milky Way and through two hundred million galaxies beyond. To an uncritical observer, Anaam was looking for freedom and justice in the twinkling light that wheeled about the universe of dark matter. But the Fatima of Fatima's dream felt deeply embarrassed by her mother's disingenuous posturing, zipping through billions of light years in search of business as usual.

Suddenly, she was woken by tugs on her shoulder and the voice of a parrot, not her sister's.

"Fatima. Fatima. Fatima."

Umar explained that he had been freed from military service because he did not, so to speak, pass the physical. He had a wine birth mark on his testicles that, according to him, was a contagious skin disease that caused impotence and apostasy. No one wanted anything to do with him.

"I don't want to die," Umar said. "By the way," he added, "mother and Rahma will be thrown off the roof of the radio station later today."

Fatima shrugged her shoulders and reconfigured her veil of cynicism. "Maybe she will fly." She added quickly, "They do the same thing to corrupt business people in the west. That explains eclipses of the sun and the moon."

Umar said he didn't know anything about that. And then he did a curious thing. He took Shaimaa into his arms for the first time since she was born and looked at her, admittedly, like leftover aubergine.

Fatima had already sensed a sea change in her brother's attitude toward gender relations. Distaste for his Sons of Ahwah captors and fear of mortification of his own flesh had opened a pathway for détente with his sisters. "Fatima," he offered, "you're mostly not a pig." It was a start.

That afternoon, snow began to fall or so it seemed. Once again, the Americans were dropping leaflets from their airplanes suggesting that everyone flee the city before imminent military assault. They, the central government and a variety of other altruistic factions promised that liberation was at hand.

"No one will go to the camps," Umar said. "At least, the Sons of Ahwah give us water and electricity."

If Fatima had political opinions, she did not share them. This one time, however, low embers of gratitude burned in her belly. According to Umar, she was *mostly not a pig*. "You are right, brother. No one will go to the camps."

And no one read the confetti as it fell from the sky. In fact, it was, ironically, festive prelude to the launching of Anaam and Rahma from the radio station roof. Fatima steered her little sister's hand toward the sky.

"Look," she said. "Your mother is preparing a lesson on gravity."

For Shaimaa, pedagogy was a ladder whose rungs were made of sand. Because of this, she was the best witness to the day's events.

But Umar feared learning or trauma where none was possible. "We will not look," he said, plucking the idiot child (so called by her mother) from the arms of Fatima. Opinion was split on the matter, but each in the crowd listened quietly as religious leaders read out the crimes and sentences.

Thereafter, when Anaam and Rahma took each other's hand and coiled somewhat in preparation to jump, Fatima thought it imprudent on her mother's part to attach her last earthbound moments to the much heavier Rahma. Obviously, she was unacquainted with Einstein's general theory of relativity, the lightness of being afforded by forgiveness nor, for that matter, the value of a human hand.

Said Umar, looking away but standing in front of Fatima, reading events in her glowing face, "How can you *watch*?"

Fatima could watch because Anaam and Rahma had already creased the air with forgotten data. "I only believe," she said, "what my eyes can't see." Similarly, the sickening sound of buckling bone produced only waves of denial. "And I only believe what my ears can't hear." Of course, she was referring to the world of her fabulous dream where pancaked flesh is no more real than a pixel of animation and every human injury is merely a comedic device.

And so, as Fatima stared at Rahma's broken legs and obvious and stupendous fractures to her mother's cervical vertebrae, she patiently awaited the recombination and flight of the capitalist whores and some fusion of slipstream and rapture that would vacuum her city from the face of the earth and up and into and beyond the contracting lungs of the universe. After all, the cycle of liberation and occupation punctuated by death and misery and false hope was no more a credible human story than Mickey Mouse and his Magic Kingdom. For confirmation of her thesis, Fatima looked at pools of blood from the mouths of Anaam and Rahma. Indeed, each looked very much like a conversation bubble for the finger of Allah. Flesh and word were cleared for takeoff.

Said Fatima to her siblings, excluding irony from her feverish visions, exposing her horse's teeth, "Our liberty has been bought with kebab and fried aubergine."

Of course, Umar and Shaimaa had no idea what their sister meant or why she chose this moment to recall their last family meal.

Hoodwinked

Patches of pink palate and wedges of nostril flap lie in surgical trays for disposal. The acrid smell of burnt flesh lingers, reminder of smoke from cauterized wounds in Louie's mouth. Momentarily, he shakes his head as he starts to come round.

Loretta enters and reacts with instinctual tenderness, begins to massage the inflammation in Louie's forearms and knees. Thereafter, her fingers grab and release folds of loose flesh the length of Louie's back, stimulate blood and lymph circulation. There's nothing to be done for the eye lost to ulceration.

Changing key, Loretta recalls a game they play, taps Louie's black nails against the operating table, creates a kind of metronome that draws him further toward consciousness. She could be a hypnotist waking someone from embarrassing collusion.

The charm bracelet on her left wrist produces incidental, tinny percussion, her call to him as powerful as a triangle cymbal at the supper hour. Her only charm reads, *Louie Loves Loretta*, and the links of the bracelet, itself, are the birthstones of each – emerald and ruby.

She thinks she said it out loud. She's not certain. *Come back to me, darling.*

But it might have been otherwise. Three days earlier, the veterinarian asks, "Have you considered putting him down?" It's an odd question, she thinks, with peculiar and unnecessary gravitas. Only after Loretta has set Louie down does she realize that Doctor Chin is channelling Macbeth - *Have you considered the innocent sleep that knits up the ravelled sleeve of care?*

She plucks Louie from the floor and screams, "Never!"

In any event, she is absent for much of Doctor Chin's argument, like a juror ignoring a prosecutor who has already lost his case. But it is not her conviction, alone, that produces absentia. The events of that morning have created perfectly counterpoised distraction.

Loretta lies naked on her four poster bed, her pillowed legs a kind of sluice gate for the tides of OM or Orgasmic Meditation. Ernesto, her *stroker*, has been massaging her clitoris for ten minutes, taking direction to go slower, lighter or in a different direction. For Loretta, OM is both acronym and onomatopoeia. She resonates as one with the universe, her body and her spirituality a two-pronged tuning fork with perfect pitch.

The problem for the obstructive airway dogs is that they are too cute for their own good. Breeders have selected animals with the biggest eyes and the funniest, flattest faces. It's the "baby schema" effect.

Loretta is riding wave after wave of orgasmic pleasure, curling, foamy tops that bubble and glide and translate force through the open sea.

But scrunched skulls and snouts leave little room for breathing. The skeletal features have changed, but the soft tissues haven't adapted with them.

Loretta puts on her robe and goes to answer the door. The woman wears a uniform and claims that she is a forest ranger. She has come to seize the cactus in the sun room, the one that Loretta has named *penis* because of its elongated, hooked shape and white flower at its pinnacle. Says Loretta, locating the flower in her mind's eye, "You can't take my penis!" She and the forest ranger hear the bedroom door close.

Your pug is a particularly sad case. He's a young, emaciated dog with laryngeal collapse or worse. He's already struggling to walk. He's lost an eye.

The plant is native to one single drainage at the bottom of the Grand Canyon. Loretta had purchased the rare cactus on eBay from a seller in the Ukraine. She had no idea that this particular specimen had been impregnated with a tracking device. Says the forest ranger, "You're in possession of stolen property and a protected species."

The constant fight to draw in air can also create a destructive negative pressure inside the animal. The stomach gets drawn into the chest. This kind of dog has a perpetual background fear of suffocation.

Loretta is reminded of rendering a butterfly in an airless jar when she was just a little girl. She cried then and now. She hands over the plant even as she parrots petulant refusal, "You can't have him."

The veterinarian feels like the devil demanding Loretta's first born, feels impugned with evil agency. "It's not what *I* want," he says. "Louie will live with fear and dread. Struggle to move and breathe and sleep. It's what's best -"

"Louie has more followers on Instagram than Madonna, Lady Gaga and David Beckham. Should I ask them what they think?"

Doctor Chin remembers Louie's neck collar with iPhone and leather phone case and Loretta's continued popularity as an actress in syndicated reruns. He is vaguely aware of the terms *trolling* and *doxing*. He swiftly arranges a time and date for the surgery.

The next day, Loretta picks up Louie and drives to the Sunset Retirement Home. It is a *horrible, horrible* place, no less so because her broken father lives there, a stroke victim whose left side has melted like carnival wax. In addition, his eyes move like windshield wipers set at the fastest speed, spasticity has given him a vulture's claw and eating and vacating his bowels are functions without relations. Regardless, Loretta visits once a month to settle accounts and dodge foul combinations of solids, liquids and gases.

But this visit is particularly unpleasant, one of those *exit visits* that Loretta dreads. Louie the First lives under water, so to speak, and only communicates with his right hand, a slate and a slate pencil. Typically, his complaints produce the same words in random order: *nurse, television, food, noise,* and the ever popular *stunk, stinks* or *stank*, to indicate events, presumably, atmospheric or particular. Lately, however, he has populated his prose with a new phrase, *down to the sea*. Loretta has pretended not to know what that means, but she knows perfectly well what that means.

When he was a beautiful and whole man, Louie the First would conduct research at the Coal Oil Point Reserve, one of the best remaining examples of coastal-strand environment. Louie the First had produced peer-reviewed papers on the raccoon round worm and collected data on migratory ocean mammals. Come the weekend, however, Louie the First would scream - *down to the sea*! - and drive the family to Coal Oil beach for a swim and a picnic. Loretta sometimes recalls these bucolic moments with word play and a double negative, "My life ain't no picnic no more."

In any event, her father's half of shared accommodation features a 10' X 6' tile mural of Louie the Second affixed to the ceiling; elsewhere, Louie the Second's image appears on a round sandstone coaster, a twelve piece puzzle (that Louie the First hasn't even opened, yet), a box of one hundred bookmarks, a silver plate, a pillow case, a duvet, a seat cushion and flip flops. Of course, the pug's mug also appears on travel accoutrements that include a dog bowl, a biscuit jar and bed linen. Loretta has already updated the digital picture frame with a slide show depicting Louie the Second's operation.

Today, the monthly selfie does not go well. Loretta notices a salt lake of slobber in the middle of her father's cleft chin. She grimaces and recoils as though she were compelled to look at child pornography. Conversely, Louie the Second has left a river of drool on the breast of Loretta's cardigan. "Poor thing" she says, visualizing his stitched epiglottis. Loretta is equally sympathetic when Louie the Second vomits pain medication and grain-free kibble. She plants kisses behind his rose ears and takes out shea butter baby wipes from her Louie Care handbag. "It's okay, sweetie," she says. "It's not your fault." In contrast, Louie the First produces wet, audible notes from his anus. These disgust his visitor.

Screams Loretta, "Horace! Get in her and clean up this shit!"

The nurse assistant deftly switches one diaper for another and informs Loretta that he has a degree in modern American literature. "You know," he says, "the poet, Donald Hall, described old age as *a ceremony of losses*."

Loretta is unmoved. "Put him in my car," she says, "and poetry is for losers." She doesn't realize that her twisted syntax is semantic gold: automobiles and free verse are Israel wrestling with God.

The light at the beach is apocalyptic, what you get with the naked eye or rose-colored glasses. Loretta immediately notices a big, dead thing half interred in the sand. A crowd stands and gawks. She plants Louie the Second in the lap of Louie the First. She pushes each in the wheelchair through the sand and toward the ocean. She is vaguely aware of a scent bubble that smells like the Sunset Retirement Home, dead and dying things and synthetic fragrance groups.

The scene creates within Loretta one of those episodes that might be described as *dissociative*, a precursor, as it happens, to a later, much larger psychological break. In any event, Loretta has travelled far from her centre and high above the fray, an eye in the ether, the lost eye, in fact, of her beloved pug.

There she is in shorts and kerchief and sunglasses standing behind the Ironman Mobility Chair and the bodies of her two Louies, one broken and leaning, the other a robust log of fur.

And there's the big dead thing drawing stares and commentary from both its fan base and apparent experts. You can't see a big top, but it's a real circus.

And there's the ocean and the sky and the sand and the highway and, presumably, the air that everyone breathes, except the big dead thing.

Effectively, when she returns to her senses, both Louies are doing their best imitation of a death rattle. Louie the First is agitated by the big dead thing on the beach. On his slate board, he has scrawled preliterate symbols.

Loretta ignores her sad, self-centered dad and tips Louie the Second onto his side in order to displace the tongue and create an airway. The death rattles continue, but she hears less fluid.

The chatter around the big dead thing is alternately informed and ignorant.

"Holy fuck!" is a visceral report, both sacred and profane.

"What is it?" someone asks.

"It's huge!"

"I think it's a seabass."

"It smells like hell."

"It's a sunfish!"

"It must be ten feet long!"

The intrepid sunfish reporter holds up his iPhone like the sword, Excalibur.

"Not just any sunfish!"

It turns out that the sunfish is a hoodwinker. This particular species has managed to stay in plain sight and out of sight for a very long time. Screams the sunfish reporter, "He's fooled everyone for millions of years!"

One man in a Lakers cap doesn't understand the vernacular, much less the explanation.

Says the iPhone reporter, scrolling and reading and paraphrasing, "If you've been fooled, then you've been hoodwinked! That's why he's called a hoodwinker!"

The man in the Lakers cap kicks the belly of the beast and opines, "Looks like we get the last laugh. Who's hoodwinking who?"

"This is interesting." The sunfish reporter reads from the iNaturalist website, "He has rarely, if ever, crossed the equator."

At this point, the temperament of the group becomes mystery dinner theatre and knock-knock joke. Why did the hoodwinker cross the equator? Guesses tumble like die at a Craps table: hunger, global warming, jammed radar, Russian interference and loneliness, to name a few. Whatever the reason, the hoodwinker isn't talking and he's not smiling, either. All of his teeth are fused. He doesn't have any teeth. He's just got a big round hole for a mouth. The cruelest joke is the very best joke told by an animal unfit to smile.

In any event, Loretta's phone rings and it's a call that she absolutely must take. She leaves Louie, Louie, the hoodwinker and the flash mob on Coal Oil beach. Nobody's going anywhere in a hurry. She mounts the sandy crest toward the car at the edge of the highway. She listens to her agent and steadies herself against the trunk of the car. Her mouth drops open.

"For chrissake, they're using your line as a *GIF*! *The joke's on you! The joke's on you!* Do you believe it? It's straight outta the show! Millions of *joke's-on-you* are already circling the globe! It's your voice, Loretta. It's your face." The agent talks about a lawsuit, residuals and royalties. He ballparks the payoff at *a dollar a click.*

Loretta closes the conversation with vitriol and prejudice, "Sue their fat asses!"

That major psychological break happens here. Afterward, the flash mob at the beach guesses murder, suicide, charity or Russian interference. Many selfie themselves into the foreground. Others withdraw further afield to capture both death scenes in one frame.

In any event, Loretta turns to rejoin Louie, Louie, the hoodwinker and the flash mob. Instantly, she is *other-worlded*, become the lost eye of Louie the Second floating above the ephemeral wreck.

Pug Eye Loretta observes the horror of Terrestrial Loretta. Both hands are over her mouth. Her knees have buckled. In three feet of water, Louie the First's Ironman Mobility Chair is on its side. Louie the First's head is under water. Louie the Second is beneath the right arm of Louie the First, all of everything drowned, save the butt and the tail. It is mortuary of biomass, steel and wheel.

And then Pug Eye Loretta surveys the tracks of the mobility chair, how they arc portside and toward the water beneath the impossible locomotion of Louie the First's left arm. And then Pug Eye Loretta witnesses the approach of the flash mob, each of these a bloodhound behind the sightline of an iPhone. And then Pug Eye Loretta inspects the abandoned hoodwinker, a fart-inflated, grey membrane with a crooked, pencil-thin smile.

And then Pug Eye Loretta does the only thing she can do. She walks back the claim that poetry is for losers, because preliterate Louie has left his blank slate in the white sand, an image file whose lossless format reads - *The joke's on you.*

Blaming Justin Bieber

His uncle woke him up with a boozy, baritone rendition of "King of the Road". Something or someone was *for sale or rent* and the speaker *ain't got no cigarettes*. Uncle Jack was on the dole because he had a bad back, a drinking problem and unpredictable employment as a bush pilot. When the cheques came out, he and his Canadian Club took a seat at the kitchen table and regaled Stephen's father who, given opportunity, imbibed like a mosquito on a moose, *to be social*, he would tell Stephen's mom. It was difficult to square Uncle Jack's reputation as a gap-toothed *bon vivant* with two divorces and a kid in juvie. But Uncle Jack liked to wax sage in the form of questions, *Can't we all just get along?* To Stephen, this seemed sensible.

In fact, Stephen saved his venom for a closer target. He peeked through the cloth curtain separating his bed from the tiny living space that abutted the smaller kitchen. He studied the droopy-eyed self-absorption of his father. His dad's hands appeared to be made of Velcro or fly paper. They stuck to the bottle and his own shot glass. More infuriating was his dad's pubescent cackle. It was like listening to a hyena vocalize glee before a ripped purse of steaming guts. Stephen tried to cotton his ears with his pillow. Nothing worked. It was a long night of penance for sins Stephen could not recount much less imagine.

But no repast is complete without dessert. Stephen awoke much later to the sight of his naked father stumbling toward the chamber pot. He was riding the arm of Stephen's mom, Gail. Their own bed was a stone's throw away and only separated from his by another of the ubiquitous curtains. Stephen often wondered why their cottage remained in the Dark Ages while all the others had air conditioning, satellite dishes and actual running water. In any event, the theatre was bad, very bad. Stephen watched, cringed and boiled as his dad pissed all over the floor, the wall and the oil stove, and his mom, pot in hand, tried to field the stream like a gold-glover.

"Jesus, Frank," she said. "Watch what you're doing!"

When he awoke for the hundredth time, he smelled immediately the industry of his mom and his Aunt Jane. He crawled to the bottom of his bed and peeked through the curtain. They were shuffling around the linoleum in the kitchen filling countertops with rows of partially cooked cabbage, steamed rice and hamburger. Tomato sauce was bubbling on the wood stove. Elsewhere, on the kitchen table, there were baskets of beets, string beans and onions. After the making of holubtsi, borscht was in the docket. Later, as per tradition, they would bring out blueberries and raspberries and make pie.

    Stephen's dad was there, too. He was in his work clothes sitting quietly on the sofa, his back to the picture window overlooking the lake. When a car horn sounded outside, he rose unsteadily and proceeded toward the door. He hovered around his wife for a parting kiss, but he never got one. He was only seconds out the door when Stephen's mom developed a text she had apparently started already.

    "I could kill him," she said. "He knows he can't handle liquor, but he likes to pretend he can. And Jack!"

    Aunt Jane punctuated her remarks by stuffing cabbage leaves with red meat. She didn't look up. "Everything's about *being a man* with them. They have no shame! In fact, Ted got into the shower with me the other day -"

    Stephen recoiled in his bed. He had a vague idea that the conversation was going to be embarrassing forthwith. It angered him to no end that adults mistook curtains for walls. He dressed quickly and appeared. "Where's dad going?" he said.

    "He got called into work. There was a storm in the city last night. Power's out." His mom looked at Barb. "Serves him right. He'll suffer."

    Aunt Jane suggested *tit for tat*, that ice water Gail *tie one on* herself. She elevated a Safeway bag with two bottles of wine in it. Aunt Jane said that Gail had already *punched her card*, that she would be *in that number, when the saints go marching in.*

    Stephen didn't listen. He went out back to what was euphemistically called *the shack,* a storage shed repurposed as a bedroom. His older brothers had bunked there during earlier summer vacations, created wallpaper of nude female pin-ups. Between Gail and her eldest, the choice of decor had been a knock-down-drag-out battle and she immediately removed the pictures when Drew and Michael started to stay home summers to work. All that remained were ghostly white rectangles, reminders of old wounds unbandaged.

Sometimes, for Stephen, the rectangles were windows upon deep feelings of shame and anxiety.

Now, one of two beds in the shack had been replaced with a small desk and a bookshelf. Stephen was already reading teenager tomes like *The Maze Runner* and *Life of a Loser*. Today, in honour of her birthday, he was recopying a freshly written poem for a girl he loved whose name he did not know. He remembers the introduction.

"Look!" her mom said. "Our son has a new little friend!"

Stephen was the *new little friend* of Muthusamy or Sammy, a boy of the same age who was quite small and precocious. "Stephen," said Sammy's mother, "this is my daughter, Kamalarani."

He was smitten immediately. All the world's butterflies shimmied in his stomach. But it was hard to court someone whose name you couldn't remember and Stephen was too embarrassed to ask her or her brother to repeat it.

The Mahadhevan family were Tamils originally from Sri Lanka. When the retired school principal died three doors down, the Mahadhevans bought the cottage as a summer retreat from Toronto. Stephen's dad said, "The Tamils from Sri Lanka speak English better than we do." Stephen's mom said, "The Tamils from Sri Lanka seem very nice." They had a Lexus, a speedboat and a fire pit.

Sammy and Stephen did most everything together for the first month of vacation. Frequently, in the large porch at the back of Sammy's cottage, the boys would wrestle in the king-sized, extra bed at one end. Stephen was taller and would pin his smaller opponent. One day, however, he found himself with his head between Sammy's thighs. He told himself he could make Sammy laugh by pursing his lips and blowing hard on Sammy's soft flesh, but his lie to himself and his breathlessness were both obvious. He saw Sammy less often after that because what Sammy knew made Stephen feel uncomfortable.

But, to a point, the fire pit was safe neutral ground. It was lit most nights by Sammy's father and Stephen and the Mahadhevan family enjoyed hotdogs or hamburgers or s'mores. One night, when just the kids were about, Sammy's sister taunted Stephen. She was three years older and she liked to kid him because he was an apostate. She could see idolatry in his eyes.

Sammy's sister held up a s'more sandwich. "What do you think, Stephen? Do you think a Tamil girl and a Canadian boy can be delicious together?"

The question confused Stephen. In the tapered fingers of Sammy's sister, the gooey confection looked like the bobbing head of a cobra.

"Do I have to draw you a map?" Sammy's sister pried open the s'more sandwich ever so slightly. "You can see," she said, smiling wryly, "how the Tamil chocolate and the Canadian marshmallow are in bed together."

The metrics of the joke were old, but Stephen didn't know any better. He leaned back in his chair because his face was burning up in proximity to the fire. Sammy's sister was giggling and Stephen hated how much he loved to look at her and listen to her laugh.

Sammy said, "If you waste a s'more, I'm going to be very upset."

Mostly, though, fire chat was the purview of Sammy's father. He had a shock of grey hair and a fleshy paunch. He liked open dress shirts over printed floral shorts. Sasitharan Mahadhevan loved Blue Jays baseball and often listened to the games on the radio around the fire pit. He was a barrister and he talked like one. Unprompted and unannounced, he would get to his feet, breathe deeply of the night air, silence chatter with an index finger to his lips and then list the reasons that he was grateful for Canadian citizenship. His family rolled their eyes, but their smiles were inclusive.

It was a different matter, however, when Sammy's dad had too much to drink. He kept a cooler full of Molson Canadian beside his lawn chair and made regular withdrawals. On those nights, Sammy's dad would sing patriotic songs of independence, songs that he had learned as one of *the boys* or Pudiyangal. This prompted his wife to claw at her husband from the edge of her chair and to plead in her own language what Stephen understood to mean, "Stop! Sit down!"

Sammy whispered to Stephen with complete detachment and even a shrug, "Maybe my dad was a terrorist. Maybe he wasn't." He extended his arms to either side, elbows bent, hands skyward, like a Shiva yogi. "Who knows?"

Sammy's sister was equally ambivalent. She surfed the air with a cobra s'more.

Stephen rose to his feet and pushed the chair under his desk. He had left the shack and returned many times. Once, he walked through Windy's Lot where the blueberries grew best; another time, he circled the canal landward of the lake lock, tossed pebbles into the shallow water and watched impassively as the suckerfish scattered. Other forays he would not remember. He looked almost entirely inward.

He had re-written the poem dozens of times, adding and subtracting the same words like beads on an abacus. He was frustrated by his lack of progress, the idea that any version of the poem was imperfect. He told himself repeatedly that his were honest feelings and that he needed to find the courage to share them. He was unware of the hubris of his strategy, packaging his feelings as a gift.

Poem in pocket, Stephen was met at the door by Sammy.

Sammy said, "Get in here. You gotta see this weird scene. It's all hell!"

Stephen didn't notice the spinach puttu, string hoppers and vegetable curry on the dining room table. He didn't read on the wall the Christmassy lettering that spelled, *Happy Birthday*. In the length of one breath, he had moved through the main room and into the back porch. Air conditioning made the room feel like cold storage.

The *weird scene* had several parts. Sammy's sister was performing a hip hop dance to a song called "Sorry" by Justin Bieber. At some points, she leapt onto the large, king-sized bed and made whirring scissors of her legs. All the while, her eyes were distant as she mouthed the choreography, *heel, toe, heel, toe, five, six, seven, eight, make a fist.*

Sammy whispered to Stephen that she was *supposed* to do a village folk dance in the costume provided by her parents. "It's a *tradition*!" His eyes popped from his head, communicated competing currents of shock and mockery. "Look at her! Can you believe it?"

Stephen looked at the rumbled blouse and petticoat in the lap of Sammy's mom, the long folds of a sari that fell over either knee like the moulted skin of a garter snake. Sammy's father sat rigid and hidden behind aviator sunglasses.

Stephen's hand reached into his pocket. His fingers closed around his poem as though he were extinguishing the light in his heart. He watched the bare midriff of Sammy's sister as he crumpled the poem into a ball. He heard *jump up, push down, groove, groove* and then play-by-play from a Blue Jays matinee. He hadn't heard the radio before.

Sammy's father went to the screened windows fronting the cottage and overlooking the lake. With his shirt sleeve, he wiped his nose and dried his eyes. Outside, the late afternoon sun and heat were oppressive, but he cranked open one of the window panels, looked at and listened to what caught everyone's attention.

Stephen's mom and Aunt Jane were whooping it up in the water, splashing and twirling and churning through the sandbar that inclined to deep water beyond. They had spent all day cooking around the woodstove and, at Jane's insistence, *rehydrating* with wine. Now, they were drunk and they were skinny-dipping and they were, to all appearances, unaware of a community of gawkers or the high afternoon sun.

Stephen was frozen with horror. He felt doubly betrayed by obscenity and abandonment.

To make matters worse, Sammy's dad turned from the window and announced to no one in particular, without judgment, what was obvious to all. "Mrs. Olynyk is three sheets to the wind. And she's naked as a jaybird."

He then looked at his wife, as if he were directing traffic at an emergency scene, and asked her to get into the small, outboard boat, to go help Mrs. Olynyk and whoever else was with her. "Make sure they're okay," he said. "Stay with them, if you can." He added, "I would do it myself, but -"

Stephen looked at Sammy, his wide eyes and half-open mouth, heard the things that Sammy didn't say, *Look at her! Can you believe it?* It was more, way more than Stephen could bear.

He did not excuse himself. When the screen door behind him recoiled on its hinge and smacked the jamb, he didn't hear it.

He walked rapidly toward home, his eyes fixed on the green grass. He had the feeling that everything was combustible, that he was made of straw and carrying fire, that he would no longer long for anything anymore and that nothing about this day or any other would ever be good in his memory or dreams.

At the Campbell camp beside his own, he veered diagonally through rocks and brush and almost fell when his ankle turned. He emerged from behind the woodshed, sped by the figure of his father in the driveway, entered the shack and threw himself onto the bed.

His father couldn't hear him crying or guess motivation for his self-absorption. In his hand was a brown paper bag full of chocolate s'mores.

Necropsy

     Soon-Yi's father was trafficked into slavery on an unregistered trawler or ghost ship. His image appeared in the *spotlight* section of the Guardian newspaper and reminded viewers of the eyes of an animal caught in a live trap. The editors ran the picture without a caption because the face, the leg iron and the net full of forage fish said it all. Shortly thereafter, Soon-Yi's mother also became a derelict soul. She would order her daughter to evacuate her bowels and bladder in a standing position. Soon-Yi's father had martyred the family for pet food and livestock feed. Someone had to pay for his lack of judgement.

     As a result, Soon-Yi ran away from her mother at the age of seven. She was often seen living out of trash cans in the shanty town of Guryong and hallooing at the moon with stray dogs. Witnesses marvelled at her athleticism and the lightness of her footfalls. She would gambol on roofs made of plywood, corrugated metal or cardboard and all produced the same sound: moccasins on linoleum. Prior to her rescue and rehabilitation, Soon-Yi did not speak a language that anyone understood. The tabloids in Seoul called her *dog girl*.

     She was sent to an orphanage run by Presbyterian clergy. After the war, the Andong Academy had welcomed the *dust of the street* or the unwanted children of Korean women and foreign servicemen. Soon-Yi's picture was hung beside those of cohorts from sixty years earlier. It did not look out of place. Of course, mothers of these *surrenders* were no less abandoned. They suffered from a kind of post-coital tristesse, shame and melancholy that lasted from five minutes to five or more decades. Those inclined to misogyny said *comfort women* should expect none and, logically, all women are comfort women.

     It was Soon-Yi's job to collect donations to the baby box behind the rectory. Under the cover of darkness, unwed mothers would leave their infants next to deliveries of milk and fresh water eel. Regrettably, Soon-Yi's celebrity was calamitous. An average of two arrivals a month hit double and then triple digits. Pastor Choi described congestion in the lane as a *spin cycle of dirty laundry*. Miraculously, prayer produced a generous gift from the defunct American Cinema down the street: queueing stanchions with blue velvet ropes, red carpet aisle runners with *Warner Brothers* insignia and one stand-alone, hand sanitizer. Thereafter, crowd control in the alley was elegant and sanitary.

Unfortunately, Pastor Choi had much in common with Soon-Yi's mother. He did not blame the girl for the explosion of orphans at the church. He blamed Soon-Yi because they, like her, were not registered in court. Undocumented babies fueled adoption taboos. To punish Soon-Yi for her invisibility, he tried to introduce her to sexual impropriety. His hand was stayed by the cry of a hundred babies. Eventually, he spoke of this on his death bed, describing Soon-Yi to his confused confessor as a "movie usher with pretentions" or, after reflection, "an animal that cannot be weaned". There was no place in his theology for divine intervention.

Seven years later, Soon-Yi impressed ice hockey scouts at a pre-Olympic tournament in Seoul. As a goaltender, she lacked rebound control, but her anticipation was uncanny. An expansion team from Canada called the Scarborough Wolves drafted her in the eighth round. Some said it was a publicity stunt to put a female on a young men's team. Others quoted Bob Dylan: *The Times They Are A-Changin'*. Her only game as a minor pro athlete produced a minor coincidence. She would one day marry one of the spectators in the crowd.

In any event, ice hockey cannot be played without ice. Cooling pipes in the arena floor failed midway through the first period of her first game. Five miles of sub-zero brine water became bath water in a matter of minutes. Referees ordered players to their dressing rooms, but Soon-Yi exited her crease, slogged through the slush and fog and collected the hockey puck at the red line. She scored once before she was physically restrained. One spectator leapt to her feet and screamed with joy. The local paper tweeted immediately, *Dog Girl Saves Wolves from Drowning.*

After her exhibition goal, Soon-Yi did not play another minute. She continued to practice with the Wolves, dress and undress in separate quarters. She was not unaware that many of her teammates looked at her as they did their pre-game meal. One morning, while sloughing off sweaty hockey pants, a sheet of paper appeared beneath the door to her change room. Soon-Yi looked at four sketches of sexual penetration between a man and a woman. One of these sketches was circled and captioned: *We think you like it doggy-style.* Soon-Yi squatted and despoiled the drawing with urine. For a variety of reasons, dreary wordplay and sexual harassment were like traffic in a shipping lane: each was predictable, unrelenting and required long distances to come to a stop.

Of course, later in life, Soon-Yi's marital partner, Joni, would retell these stories in a voice that was alternately singsong or deadpan. One could believe that Soon-Yi had lived the life of the man-cub, Mowgli, of *Jungle Book* fame, all cartoon resourcefulness, nothing morbid or mortal. It was not Joni's fault. Soon-Yi was a Google search with a million capillaries. People looked to Joni to shrink-wrap the kernel of this fantastic story. It was important work, but drudgery, too. Joni felt like a dishwasher in a soup kitchen.

In contrast, their first meeting in Toronto was a feeding frenzy. Joni remembers Soon-Yi sitting front and centre in her adult ESL class. She remembers how her new pupil convulsed like an inflatable air dancer whenever she wanted to answer a question. Joni invited Soon-Yi to stay after class one evening and discovered that her delight in one thing was delight in all things. They enjoyed the kind of sex that made each feel like a conjoined porpoise. They banged and banged and banged against whiteboards and wireless access points. Afterward, Joni gushed, "I saw you at the Wolves game." Soon-Yi said, "And now you see me without my mask." Six hours later, a custodian woke them with a commercial floor scrubber.

Regrettably, their marriage drew misgivings on Joni's side of the family. The *dog girl* thing was the trending topic, but Joni heard darker business behind the headline: prejudice against gender, sexual orientation, ethnicity and even their choice to remain child-*free* as opposed to child-*less*. Joni's grandmother – a self-described *maverick* - misquoted Roseanne Barr, communicated cynicism or ignorance or devilry: "The thing women have yet to learn is that nobody gives you power. You just *fake* it." In any event, Joni had to bear this animus all by herself, because Soon-Yi's experiences were like solitaire, both a game and a gem. For Joni, the rigours of self-defence reflected the slow course of a solar eclipse. The terrain between her and her lover was sometimes dark and cold.

The trip to a beach in Prince Edward Island was framed by Joni as a *quest*. They would help save a whale drowning in shallow water. Said Joni, "I think her radar is discombobulated or maybe she was injured by a ship. It's always an accident, you know. It's always the *whale's* fault." Soon-Yi laughed and described the trek to the east coast as a *budget junket*. She said it had more to do with their massive credit card debt after trips to Amsterdam and Rio de Janeiro. But Joni insisted otherwise, "Okay, we're vacationing closer to home this time, but it has nothing to do with *broke bitch syndrome*." In fact, Joni longed to reach out to the whale like a mother goddess and to reorient its suicidal compass. Soon-Yi would not say what she felt, that beneath her own humor and bluster was some kind of rip tide.

    They never met the owners of the Seafarer B&B. At midnight, a sticky note on the unlocked front door read, *Welcome Joni and Soon-Yi!* On the breakfast table the next morning, they discovered warm *toutons*, a Newfoundland treat of bread dough fried up like pancakes. Joni tried hers with molasses while Soon-Yi smothered a stack with both molasses and maple syrup. Before they left, Soon-Yi said the owners of the B&B must be *seafarers*, themselves, of no fixed address. Joni remembered a poem of the same name by Ezra Pound, lines that read, "Bitter breast-cares have I abided / Known on my keel many a care's hold". She did not say the lines out loud.

    At the entry to Basin Head beach, Joni and Soon-Yi held hands briefly and then broke right and left to reconnoiter. It was some time before they realized they were going in opposite directions. Joni became annoyed and turned first. "Where's the whale?" she screamed. "I don't see the whale!" Soon-Yi began to narrow the gap between them and pointed in the direction of the ocean, but Joni was already reading a huge sign on two metal stakes: *Dogs must be leashed at all times. No lifeguards. Swim at your own risk.* These informational bullets were juxtaposed with a promotional paragraph. "Hey," said Joni, "have you ever heard of *silica*? This beach has singing sands!" Arm in arm, they leapt from the boardwalk. Synchronous footfalls produced squeaks that sounded like mice.

    Once they had stopped, Joni pressed her hand on Soon-Yi's shoulder. She said the singing sands reminded her of the singing mermaids from mythology. "They were like you, hot chicks with big boobs. And they lured passing sailors to their deaths." Joni added, "Do you think any of those mermaids were gay?" She laughed and answered her own question. Each and every one was gay. The evidence spoke for itself. "Of course," she said, "we all end up in

Davy Jones' Locker. Hetero men leave the light on for lesbo fishes. You know it, girl!"

Maybe Soon-Yi wanted to laugh, but her attention was drawn elsewhere. From a bend further up the beach, a small dog approached at breakneck speed. Joni curled defensively behind Soon-Yi. The dog hurtled into Soon-Yi's leg, rebounded, fell onto one side and then righted itself. It shook out the loose parts on its head: thick, black flews over its lower jaw and bat ears, broad at the base, tapered and round at the top. Thereafter, it leapt into Soon-Yi's arms and squirmed like a marlin exiting the sea. Soon-Yi endured a torrent of licking and then held the animal at arm's length. It had no collar or tags. "Look at that face!" screamed Joni. It was a dark-eyed crater. Soon-Yi set the dog down. The animal retreated quickly and disappeared further up the beach. Joni was flush with excitement: "That's one suicidal dog!"

The track of a barbecue grill led them to the awful scene around the bend. The whale they had come to save was actually long dead, the majority of its bones already flensed of fat and skin. Soon-Yi grimaced and pinched her nostrils. They had penetrated a scent bubble of fecal matter, poached organs and rotten blubber. An ovary lay in the sand and a neat row of teeth formed a half-smile. Groups of competing interests shared comfort zones and points of view. Locals talked about the rash of right whale deaths and debated the impact of fishing gear entanglements or blunt force trauma in shipping lanes. Tourists took selfies with the lone, remaining whale eye. A mixed group lined up for burgers at the barbecue.

The largest numbers belonged to scientists from the Royal Ontario Museum. Some were collecting DNA samples. Others were crating bones in manure. Most wore rubber boots, rubber gloves and rain pants. The chief curator was doing an interview with the media and described her work as a *necropsy*. In response to a question, she said, "The tail has very powerful muscles and they're very hard to remove." She held in her hand a knife whose blade was a metre long. Other knives had been sharpened so often that they resembled a smaller shank or shiv.

Joni was frozen in place, her devastation bundled with self-reproach. How, exactly, had she expected to save the whale? And how long ago had she learned of the whale's distress? Evidence was everywhere that Joni had been sleepwalking. Indeed, she had forgotten to fill the gas tank and she and Soon-Yi had stalled on the highway. She had also forgotten the sex toys in the box beneath the bed. That big, greasy fart of a whale and that empty gas tank and those idle toys were all a plumb line to the bottom of the sea. Joni realized that her *errors* had been *decisions*. She wasn't trying to save her marriage. She was trying to scuttle it. Joni wanted to waken and forget.

As for Soon-Yi, she did not reflect upon the crash site. Rather, she watched the small dog leap from whale chunk to whale chunk. She listened to the skid of paws in puddles of grease, soft friction that sounded like moccasins on linoleum. Suddenly, someone threw a stone or a pine cone. Soon-Yi heard, "It's not right." Whether from instinct or impact, the dog catapulted onto the beach and ran down a Frisbee in mid-air. The owner of the Frisbee immediately cut his friend out of the loop. The small dog ran and ran and ran and leapt and caught and retrieved. Now, the boy was launching the Frisbee into the ocean. Over and over again, the small dog pursued its quarry into the water and returned the disc to its owner.

Joni was watching the dog and Soon-Yi's face. Joni was the first to articulate fear. "Oh, no," she whispered. The boy had performed a sleight of hand trick, feigned throwing the Frisbee far into the ocean and hid it behind his back. The small dog swam the impossible trajectory of the boy's hand, churning his little legs, scouring the horizon and always breathing once more before his last. Most everyone spectated and judged. Some said *poor dog* or *stupid dog*. Others described the boy as *evil* or *depraved*. One man used obscenity to deputize the whole crowd: "Where the *fuck* is that dog's owner?"

Joni forgave the boy because he was having fun and didn't know any better. She wanted to comfort him, but she and the others could no longer move or exhale. They were suddenly transfixed by clear skies, light winds and Soon-Yi, the eyewall.

Of course, she had already stripped. She was wading into the surf and in the direction of the dog. Onlookers experienced a kind of false equivalence. Soon-Yi's nudity and the peril of her mission produced equal amounts of terror and awe.

In very little time, the dog's head became a compass point. Still, Soon-Yi swam further and deeper, her arms cutting the waves and her long, black hair undulating in breaking, white foam. At the moment that Soon-Yi used her powerful leg muscles to kick and dive, Joni knew she had an error or a decision to make, singing sands or singing sirens and what would she do for want of forgotten things?

An Infinite Game

Our executioner combined the qualities of a wag and libertine, parading his sociopathy as an out-sized clown.

The bayonet attached to his rifle was exceptionally long, a sawback with a broad, flat blade. The press catch was at the nine o'clock position. This particular bayonet would be a poor weapon in close combat, but, in the field, as an instrument of summary murder, no one would question its utility.

According to the executioner, the four of us would stand front to back and in close formation. The one of us at the end of the line and inviting the initial impact and de-acceleration of the weapon would surely die. The second was, too, a strong candidate for a death certificate. The third in line would be conflicted, good odds for survival undermined by exceptions to good odds for survival. At the top of the line was Pinocchio, someone who would likely live to be human.

Each of us was instructed to draw a lot consisting of straw from a corn broom, the shortest sealing the fate of the first and so on. Three of us, including myself, were spare of build. The fourth man had a great fleshy paunch and the teats of a large, lactating animal. There wasn't one of us, political correctness aside, who did not pray to be seeded behind his reserves of sloth and appetite.

The large man won the lottery part of the game and sure salvation. Fate saw humanity where the rest of us only saw pockets of insulation. Nonetheless, I was only marginally less fortunate and, as a result, pressed my chest between the large man's shoulder blades. The two men aligned behind me were, as I saw it, earmarked for the hereafter.

I had heard about human beings surviving rods and bars thrust through their skulls as a result of industrial accidents or rough play. I wondered if such a miracle were empirically possible with a violent intrusion into the torso. The one who had lost the lottery outright, obviously not a gambler nor a student of medical oddities, suddenly broke rank and was shot through the head.

I realized then that another man's cowardice or dignity was to play a large part in my own survival. With one of us eliminated from the competition, I immediately assumed the second position. The tall man behind me was now fully exposed. He, too, must have shared my epiphany vis-à-vis men's actions and their spoils. I now smelled the effects of his subversive bowels and followed the meandering path of urine around one of my boots.

Being moved a body width closer to annihilation, I, nonetheless, experienced the faint, desperate hope of my predecessor and wondered if he, too, might break rank, if he, too, hadn't adopted the psychological character of *his* predecessor. I decided to sound out his feelings on the matter while our executioner joined a comrade on the perimeter to rest from labor and to share a cigarette.

Said the tall man, whispering in the vein of gallows humour, "I was an atheist, but now I will give myself to God."

I was less interested in his spiritual recidivism and its ironic tone and more interested in what, exactly, that meant for me. I turned my head slightly and asked the man to forego philosophy a moment and tell me what he intended to do.

"I won't be slaughtered," he said. "I, too, would rather die with a bullet in my head than be butchered like a sheep."

On a practical level, this was disturbing news. The crap in the tall man's pants was clearly a threat to his self-concept. Perhaps he believed that execution was a challenge to his personal freedom, that martyrdom, of this reckless sort, was his clearest and best, existential choice. "Millions," I whispered, "have met their maker with calm resolve, forsaken flesh for spirit." I informed the man that he might better preserve his dignity by laughing at the power of his oppressor and staying put. He mumbled a non-committal reply that served notice that war was, indeed, a better fit for me than persuasive speaking.

Fortunately, my survival instinct was whetstone to a greater strategy than naked self-interest. I decided to include *myself* in the quadrant of his ruminations, both as an individual and as a representative of his relationship with all men. First, however, I had to address the large man in front of me who kept parroting away – "What are you saying? What are you talking about?"

"Stay out of it!" I whispered, forcefully. "Shut up. *Shut up!*"

It was important that the large man assimilate my rebuke quickly since the executioner was halfway through his cigarette.

I now focussed my attention on the human riddle behind me, whispered into the no man's land that was our crucible of fear. I asked his name in order to feign interest in his identity.

"Omar" he said.

A few bits of information about his unit informed me that we were sometimes allies, sometimes not, depending upon which side had greater hardware and was prepared to use it.

Suddenly, the large man was at it again, social exclusion breeding, no doubt, mistrust in his fellow men. "What are you talking about? What are you saying?" These were complicating pin pricks in the perfectly patterned pin cushion of my ruse.

I asked the large man if I had not already explicitly told him to shut up. "Stop *annoying* me," I snarled. I assumed and conveyed moral authority because he was an easy victim of social prejudice. Besides, his identity meant nothing to me. He had nothing to offer.

I returned attention to the human riddle behind me and said the following: "You are free to preserve your own conscience in whatever death you choose, but how much better are you than they for making that decision for me?" I pointed gravely at the corpse already on the ground, both to telegraph my grim end and to reacquaint him with important imagery that he was clearly trying to avoid.

At that moment, our executioner approached us, bayonet at the ready, circling, I supposed, for dramatic effect. It struck me, and for the first time, oddly enough, that I was very likely to die whatever the thought processes of the tall man, that my own scheming and plotting and trying to win advantage were a puppet show of vanity and abstraction compared to, as we soldiers say, realities on the ground. Nevertheless, my human gift for spinning and weaving theories continued apace. I wondered if I shouldn't look at my executioner. Might he be moved by an absorbing performance of submission or contempt? Should I take a more strategic tack, ask for a new lottery given the removal of one of the original participants?

While I was evaluating costume for the stage, our executioner broke the fourth wall. He launched the bayonet clean through the large man and left me and the riddle-cum-hero unscathed. He then informed us that his reasoning was thus: "Any line of like points really has no beginning or end. As a result," he said, "I can have a go where fancy would."

Immediately, I rebutted these remarks, spoke over and above the self-interested imprecations of the tall man.

I informed the executioner that beginning and end had, indeed, been decided through the providential drawing of lots. I advanced the idea that a good referee does not change rules or *fancy* outcomes like a weathervane.

The executioner was not a parliamentarian, said that *tricks* of my sort would not stay his chosen direction, that the theatre of war was, indeed, his for the making. "It is your fault," he said, "for liking my boots for your feet."

The tall man had heard and seen enough, shit and piss once again more real than *value theory*. He bolted, knocking me forward as he did, and was summarily shot in the head.

Trembling with fear of my own, surveying the human carnage, I queried the executioner. "Why are you using that ancient weapon?" I said. "Here, in the cradle of civilization, we have all the weapons of modern warfare."

The executioner shrugged his shoulders, explained to me that *Bayonet Attack* is another name for the *King's Indian Defence*. I was dumbfounded. Did the executioner believe prisoners of war game pieces?

"Nobody dies playing chess," I said.

"It's all a game," he said. "Now, get out."

I straddled self-possession and self-abandonment, heard at my back in diminishing volume, "No beginning. No end. An infinite game."

The conceit was superficial. Our executioner was both powerful and banal. War always puts the lie to *game theory*, the idea that human activity can be reduced to mathematical models. Unless, of course, you take the largest view of boys and games and the one question that dooms us all: *can I play?*

Cicada

When grandpa was naked, I didn't see his doohickey. I was on the porch an' his belly hung big an' low like a melon.

Mama said, "For the love of God, Charlie..." She called her dad *Charlie* 'cause she said he weren't no dad o' hers.

Cliff, Mom's sleep-over friend, said, "Is he drunk?"

It weren't that simple, mama said, on account o' grandpa bein' off his rocker an' it weren't a real sure read to say liquor was come to play.

So mama hadn't seen Charlie for ten years but his showin' up naked in the twilight of the front yard was just another rusted link in the great chain o' misery. Some people never laugh or smile. My mama never knew surprise from ordinary after daddy left. He took off with the savings an' the red-headed hairdresser at *Veronique's Cuts and Shaves*. For three years, mama turned down the sheets regular-like an' set an extra place, admittin' no surprise. Then Cliff come an' moved into the spaces where daddy used to be an' the neighbors said there'd be no surprise in that house.

"What are you doin' here?" mama said to her daddy.

"I'm readyin' to fly."

Mama didn't say pea turkey 'bout that. She said, "Missy, get fixin' for bed." And I knew better to argue.

Cliff didn't say pea turkey but when he was hungry or annoyed. "What are yuh gonna do with that old, naked fart?"

I bust a gut when I heard that. *Old naked fart!* Cliff looked at me like one of those lions that kills the babies o' him that was before.

Mama said, "He can sleep in the barn. More blankets than Frank Junior needs." Frank Junior was our horse. He was born o' the union of his mama, World's Fair, and a traveling salesman named Frank. My mama says there's no other explanation. Three hundred an' forty days later from cock's crow to cock's crow. She wasn't surprised.

We left grandpa cross-legged an' naked in the yard. He's got teats like a boar hog an' long white bunches o' hair an' arms an' legs skinnier than a cricket's.

Of a sudden, grandpa raises his fist at the lot of us, says, "I don't give a dried apple damn!" *Hallelujah*, I think.

So, I'm out an hour later sittin' with grandpa under the crab tree. I get naked 'cause fair's fair.

Grandpa looks at me and says, "I can hear the nymphs. I hear their song from the earth."

That's just crazy luck, 'cause my teacher, Miss Johnson, told us once that nymphs are beautiful girls asleep in trees an' things. But grandpa says I got my nymphs all wrong. He's talkin' bugs an' he tells me the story of the cicada nymphs that spend seventeen years underground eating tree roots before livin' as winged adults for only a few weeks. "I've been lost for seventeen years," he says, "and now I am come home to be re-born."

I tell grandpa that mama says he's been away for ten years. He seems puzzled by this, like he figures the number of spokes in the wheel was a done deal.

"Missy," he says, "nothin's true but believin' makes it so."

"Halleluiah," I say. "Jane Piccolo stole my butter pecan once an' her sayin' it was hers a thousand times made everyone think it were so."

"Missy," he says, "you and I are gonna make a world of myth and Jane Piccolo and her lies can go to hell."

What with a word like *myth*, grandpa sure has a funny way o' talkin'. His eyes bug out an' he's amazed. I take a shine to grandpa. What with daddy gone and Cliff and Sneaky Pete down the road, I was thinkin' like mama that men were last in line at creation. They got a bolt o' lazy and a pound o' selfish which means they're always in a bad mood on account o' wantin' things an' never liftin' a finger to get 'em.

But grandpa's different. "Missy," he says, "it's time to build the temple." So, he gets up an' walks over to the barn to fetch what it is he needs. It's dark as molasses in there, but I can hear him movin' and movin' things. Sure enough he comes out dragging' a tangle o' chicken wire an' God Almighty he's got cutters, too.

That's when all hell breaks loose. I was jus' thinkin' about Sneaky Pete an' there he is in the road before the yard with a fishing pole in one hand an' a jar o' leeches in th' other. He's out for catchin' more o' them cats than he should, sneakin' 'em away in the dark. Anyway, he looks at me an' grandpa an' then runs an' grabs me by the arm an' pulls me toward the house raisin' a god awful racket.

And mama and Cliff come down and everyone's angry as the devil. Cliff an' Sneaky Pete say grandpa's a pervert an' I shouldn't be naked with 'im.

Mama says, "He's a lot o' things, but *that* he ain't."

Cliff says, "A man's desires change."

Sneaky Pete says, "Temptation is what made the crow fly."

I can go to my room or take a lickin'. From my window, I see Cliff in front of grandpa an' I hear the words *son of a bitch* an' Cliff pushes grandpa, leaves 'im sittin' beside the wire an' the cutters, like he wouldn't piss on 'im if he was on fire. *Big show*, I think. *Big show, Cliff.* I can barely see mama. She's standin' tall with one hand to her mouth, like a trunk cut through with lightning. I can't see her face. I don't imagine there's any surprise, anyway.

The next morning, I'm listenin' in secret to mama. She's tellin' Cliff in the kitchen that her daddy ran a junkyard an' fancied himself an inventor, used to be handier than a pocket on a shirt. Story had it he was God-fearin' once an' then he stopped believin' when the last o' the litter was born without arms an' legs an' a brain. He took to talkin' to himself an' walkin'. And walkin' and talkin' got 'im lost for ten years.

"Everybody breaks different," mama said.

I scarf my cornmeal an' grab my book bag for school an' go outside and God Almighty grandpa's built himself a huge bug statue outta wire. He's sittin' in the middle of it naked like it were a flying machine an' I remember what he said about fixin' to fly.

"Good morning, Missy," he says. "You'll be seeing a few changes around here. Hurry home if you're of a mind to witness the transformation."

*

I loved my teacher, Miss Johnson. She showed me to write *himself* for *hisself*, said I could go to college 'cause I sop like bread. She was young an' she came from the city to replace Miss Carswell who had a breakdown. Miss Johnson dressed in clothing that was soft an' colourful an' she smelled like lilac. And all the boys were in love with 'er, too. Even though they were mostly stupid an' mean, all she had to do was look at 'em an' it was like Sunday School, Jesus puttin' out his hand an' tossin' the demons outta the pigs.

Anyway, that year, Miss Johnson taught us about evolution an' I was real curious 'cause Jill Patterson piped up an' said that her daddy said that evolution is a lie an' anyone who believes it is a *prostitute*.

Well, Miss Johnson bust a gut when she heard that an' because we all wanted to please Miss Johnson, we all bust a gut. But Miss Johnson stopped quick an' said she was sorry. I never heard a teacher say that. And Miss Johnson said we needed to keep an open mind about evolution.

And it *was* the most amazin' thing. We pushed the desks back an' she brought a kiddy pool out o' the coat room an' filled it with water that she colored green with dye an' then we all got a chance to throw seeds in, bird and corn an' the like, an' then Miss Johnson put a green paper shade over the desk lamp an' asked me to turn out the lights an' then she said to get the dinosaur an' animal toys that we got from cereal boxes at the Hardware on Main an' stand 'em up around the floor an' while we did that, Miss Johnson put on a record called "The Lion Sleeps Tonight" that came all the way from South Africa an' we all sang the "wimoweh" part an' it was the right song, what with family startin' in the swimmin' hole in Africa for all of us.

"The world was once a big bowl of soup over 4.5 billion years ago," Miss Johnson says. "All life evolved from the sea. Natural selection meant that the stronger species survived."

So, we're all dancin' an' singin' *wimoweh* to "The Lion Sleeps Tonight" an' some o' the boys are playin' *animal fights* around the big soup to see who would live an' who would die an' then Principal Early comes in an' asks to talk to Miss Johnson an' she goes away an' comes back forever later. And you could see that she had been cryin' an' the rest of the day was like a funeral for God knows why.

We didn't get a lotta evolution after that. Miss Johnson told us that God created the earth in six days an' that the sun was created after an' the whole thing took about 10,000 years. And then there was the garden an' Adam an' Eve an' lickety-split a whole heap o' trouble on account o' God hoggin' the apple tree for himself. You could see that her heart wasn't in it. She read time to time from the same book I seen in Sunday school.

I asked Miss Johnston if she believed in the idea of the soup or the idea of the garden. "What's goin' on, anyway?"

Miss Johnson bit her lip an' hesitated. Finally, she said, "I will speak the truth." The truth had some relationship with the door 'cause she kept lookin' at it while she talked.

"People create what are called *myths*" she said.

I hollered, "My *grandpa's* makin' a myth! He thinks he's a grasshopper!"

It weren't exactly true, but Miss Johnson was dead serious. "Myths are stories that people believe in to comfort themselves. People are afraid. They need to believe there is an obvious reason for everything. There was no garden," she said. "No Adam and Eve. No apple tree of special importance. It's just a myth. It's not true." And then Miss Johnson reaches into the cupboard under the sink, her eyes never leavin' the door. Out comes a kinda model with monkey an' human-like shapes on pins. An' from one end to the other they get taller an' straighter.

Miss Johnson clears her throat and says, "Today, I am going to tell you the story of *Lucy*."

*

The day grandpa come, I was walkin' home cryin' 'cause Principal Early said that Miss Johnson went away an' she wouldn't be coming back. Miss Johnson had important business back in the city. We knew that was a bald-faced lie, 'cause there was adults goin' in an' outta the school an' meetin' with Principal Early an' they looked like packs o' wild dogs. An' Miss Johnson wouldn't leave without sayin' goodbye. An' God's my witness Principal Early smelled like hooch.

And if that don't beat all, I turn left at the John Deere and there's a mob in the road at my house, like it were a fair or a funeral. I drop my book bag and skedaddle. Grandpa's crouched naked an' high in the apple tree. An' he's painted himself like the cicada. He's mud-black with orange body stripes 'cept for his back where the stripes don't meet but sorta wander south toward his butt. An' God Almighty, he ain't alone in that tree. It's covered with adult cicada jus' like he said. And folks are sayin' it's not to be believed. They come once every 17 years and this makes 10, tops. And Sneaky Pete says, "There's only one way to explain it." And grandpa sees me an' he waves like it were a picnic.

"Missy," he says, "I waited for you. The time has come." And he tells me matter-of-fact that when he wore pants, he had pockets with the right papers in 'em 'bout the myth of the cicada. And I should read up on it when he's done his two weeks o' singin' an' flyin'.

And I look behind me at mama and Cliff. Cliff's got his lips puckered like he were gonna spit crab apple juice, but mama? She jus' stands there starin' at her daddy like he's a ghost.

An' God Almighty if he don't start singin'! An' Sneaky Pete says, "That sparks o' the real Mckoy. That's *real* good. It's your male," he says, "that's got the mating sounds. The female don't got a voice." He adds, "There's two weeks o' peace in the home."

An' then the whole tree is alive with the song o' the cicada. An' grandpa, maybe once in 10 or 17 years, has got 'imself a place in this world.

An' I'm watchin' mama as grandpa prepares to fly. An' what I hear next is an awful *smack* and – I'm sure of it – one less voice in the chorus. And what mama's got on her face ain't nothin' like horror or when your breath goes with sadness or shock. Mama looks surprised, like all her expectations were contrary an' the fact of it were hard up against her feelings 'o doubt. An' God if I didn't know it outright, but Cliff's days were numbered. *Hallelujah.*

*

In March of a much later year, the almond trees slumbered beneath a hoarfrost whose delicate embroidery threatened but did not subdue the bees and the blossoms; my second son called Charles was born in the company of his father and my mother; and Miss Patricia Johnson tapped me on the shoulder in the Easter chocolate aisle of Walmart. Oh, how my heart leapt! She was as a cordial to my supplicant in the temple of childhood worship, a soul in bliss, sweetly perfumed, elegant as Roman antiquity, principled as rain.

"Missy," she said. And we remembered high school graduation when she was still as a picture against the gym wall.

Of course, inevitably, our talk turned to Principal Early. The gardens darkened in her eyes and the declension of her lips was immediately twisted with the stabbing and thrusting of her wet tongue.

"Oh," she hissed, "he screwed me over, he did." And even though I stop listening, I still hear the words, *son of a bitch.*

A Night at the Oprah [sic]

Rigoletto

Randy plays the role of Gilda as an all-American girl. She has white-faced her black skin, dyed her hair blond and inserted blue contact lenses. She has even created freckles - using brow products - by bouncing the pen across her nose and cheeks. She will greet her friends at the door with joyful responses to their costumes - "Jeepers!" and "Gee Whiz!" It matters not that each is identical to the other as the hunch-backed and dour, Rigoletto. Collectively, they are a harem of pullover tunics with jagged hemlines and sewn-in foam humps. Rope belts are a full eight feet long. Randy as Gilda toys with the idea of grabbing those ropes and reimagining herself as Aphrodite, clam-glider on an ocean swell. Anyway, it is the job of all the Rigolettos, the father's job, to go down on their daughter. Randy says that it's not enough that he, her father, see her die *tragically*, as in the original. Too many old white farts have gotten that kind of *mea culpa* followed by curtain closing applause. No, Randy as Gilda has planned greater abasement for her father's sins. All the Rigolettos in the room will do what they have always done best, use their tongues as swords of malice. Ergo, when the dogs descend upon her loins, Randy as Gilda experiences waves of empowerment and restitution. But the victory is Pyrrhic, at best. All the Rigolettos in the room substitute tumescence for penance, their foam humps engorged with blood. If Randy had not white-faced her black skin, she would have predicted this result for her all-American sister. Women can't win for losing in a world of method acting.

Il trovatore

In this version of the story, Randy plays the role of Manrico, a knight and troubadour. She develops her character using a technique called *double-layering*. She wears out-sized junk to simulate a quarterstaff (strapped on with buckles and Velcro) and she conceals very little of it with a small poetry chapbook. No one should have any illusions about Manrico's goals in life and his *modus operandi*. The furry manacles on his wrists indicate that he is powerless and requires a savior, but this, too, is a ruse. All the guests dress as Leonora. Because Leonora cannot have Manrico's junk (not yet, anyway), she has *taken the veil*. She and the other nuns form a procession at Randy or Manrico's door. One of the nuns has a speaking part, says, "Lord, thy mercy on this soul." But the cuffs aren't coming off by themselves and nobody is lifting a finger. This is the part where another Leonora takes Manrico's quarterstaff into her mouth and swallows poison in order to free her lover. It's a faithful re-enactment of the original and you really have to see Leonora's ecstasy to appreciate how deeply invested she is. In the final scene, Randy playing Manrico removes his cuffs with no effort at all and ravages the remaining Leonora clones. It turns out *they all look alike* is not a racist trope but admission on the part of men that most will *foam hump* anything that moves. Ergo, Randy as Manrico must stay in character like *deus ex machina* or the great and powerful Oz.

Katya Kabanowa

On that night, Randy plays the role of Katya, a transgender who has chosen the role of a six year old boy. This is because her childhood backstory includes chastisement for disrespect and misplaced emotions, the same kind of darts she gets as a married woman leading a double life. Randy as Katya dresses very much like the wooden boy, Pinocchio. At first, her limbs don't feel like her own. It's awkward and complicated. It doesn't help that Tichon, her husband, tells her exactly how to move and what to say. No one knows if it's class, patrimony or Russian fashion that gives Tichon his sense of entitlement. Anyway, Randy as Katya playing a six year old transgender boy is cared for by her father, Boris. He is wearing hip waders and carries a Predator fishing rod in one hand. On the other hand, he has a baseball glove. To complete the boy's skill set, Boris will teach him how to ride a stationary bicycle. It's a valuable life lesson.

An old fresh face in this production is Discretion, yet another male in drag with a birch rod and a spanking fetish. Truth be told, Discretion's decision to wear blackface is a piece of inspired staging. Has it been about *race* all along? Is the binary world of white/black, Discretion/Shame too great a yoke for Randy, our African-American heroine? It would appear so, because Randy playing Katya as a six year old transgender boy is about to fall on his sword, so to speak. She climbs into the Jacuzzi while Discretion trips the light switch repeatedly to simulate a storm. Of course, while Katya slips beneath the watery berm, Tichon and Boris add their own tears to the mix because, as Discretion knows, there is no greater sacrifice than that of the common good.

More things to know about the original Pinocchio (the one that Randy as Katya hasn't already drowned in the tub): he floats and won't be drowning any time soon. He has no *woody*, so to speak, but his nose grows when he lies. He's already a boy and he doesn't know it.

Norma

Of course, Randy will play the role of Norma. It's her house, her party, her rules. *Of course*, Randy will end up dead. Most female leads in operas end up dead or crazy. That's the whole point! Randy's friends knew that when they got their evite on Facebook. Yes, there's some kind of hierarchy here, but somebody's got to take the bull by the horns and lop off its balls. If anyone codifies Randy's choices using the word *black* just once, Randy with have a bloody stroke!

Alright, Randy as Norma has great power as a Druid priestess, but everyone knows on an intuitive level that her own identity is the seed of her own destruction. Ergo, she takes the name of *Norma Jeane* (aka Marilyn Monroe). She wears a knock-off of the Jean Louis gown worn by Monroe as she sang Happy Birthday to President John F. Kennedy. Randy, as Norma (Jeane), has two children with the Roman, Pollione, but he, Pollione, is schlepping another priestess, Adalgisa. Neither woman knows of Pollione's betrayal. This is demonstrated neatly in the sex scene. His two mistresses wear blindfolds while the three commingle in a kind of mating ball. Because they *see* nothing, Pollione can argue that their other senses are dulled by the absence of one. No cheating. No harm. No foul. Historically, this argument has worked out just fine. It isn't until Adalgisa witnesses Norma (Jeane) getting a presidential enema that both women realize they are being hosed.

At that moment, Randy moves the party into the backyard for Act II. There, she has constructed a large wooden effigy or *wicker man*, a tidy bit of straw and twine that will house the sacrificial victim. Randy as Norma (Jeane) spritzes barbecue lighter fluid on the wicker man and tosses a match with her last line: "May this awful moment now show you the heart you betrayed and lost." The interesting thing here is that it is unclear if she is speaking to Pollione or Adalgisa.

Nevertheless, as the courtyard lights up with flames, Norma (Jeane) hides herself behind the inferno to indicate her own (of course) sacrifice for the perceived sins of everyone. She removes her Monroe mock-up and tosses it into the flames. The original had 2,500 hand-stitched crystals. Norma's replica has thousands of kernels of popcorn. Suddenly, the night air is like an Orville Redenbacher wet dream. A dozen people in the condo complex call the cops. Conversely, women are compelled to self-immolate every day and no one picks up the phone.

Tosca

The opera season closes with a homophone, of sorts - *A Night at the Oprah* [sic]. Randy will play the role of Tosca, but she and everyone else will dress as Oprah Winfrey in knock-off merchandise from the People's Republic of China. Ironically, American and Chinese women confirm for each other that the bourgeoisie and the proletariat are, in fact, one. Anyway, Randy as Oprah towers in glittery pumps and cuts a curvy silhouette in a form-fitting navy midi dress by Atelier Versace, the same dress worn by Oprah as Oprah at the premiere of *A Wrinkle in Time*. Randy's lover, Mario, stuns everyone with a custom-made Atelier Versace off the shoulder, long-sleeved black velvet gown with Swarovski crystal-encrusted accents along the neckline and waist. It is the same outfit worn by Oprah as Oprah when she said *time is up* for sexual predators and accepted the Cecil B. DeMille Award for outstanding contributions to the world of entertainment. Apparently, predation and entertainment are bedfellows. Who knew? Anyway, Randy as Tosca as Oprah is a little jealous of her friend and lover, Billy as Mario as Oprah, which is understandable since Mario as Oprah has since enjoyed ten million views on YouTube for her performance at the Golden Globes. Anyway, that particular tension is a good fit for the show, since Randy as Tosca suspects infidelity on the part of Billy as Mario. It is interesting to note that Billy as Mario (cue the bromance) suffers torture to protect his best male friend's location, while Randy as Tosca cannot suffer Mario's torture and must reveal the secret. This is called Uranus Joke Zero or the old mother/earth meme that vaginas suffer poor moisture resistance and cannot compete with the interior finish of a knotty pine. In any event, in this particular production, Billy as Mario mortifies the whole building with his banshee screams from the ensuite bathroom. A hockey player in 4D suspects it is a man who *screams like a girl*.

Of course, the highlight of the evening is the death scene (*Oy, vey.* Randy has barely encrypted any of these messages.) Randy as Tosca as Oprah is distraught that her lover, Mario, has been executed in an act of betrayal. Turns out, their pardon from the man that sexually abused Tosca isn't worth the sheepskin he used to write and penetrate. As a result, she (and, forcibly, everyone else) must leap to her death from the parapet of the Castel Sant'Angelo (the balcony of Randy's condo). But all the Oprahs in attendance are reluctant. Each remembers the wicker man inferno, leers and pick-up lines from first responders and the very real possibility of suffering beyond the pale. Randy as Tosca as Oprah assures everyone that there is a shock-absorbing foam landing pad three stories down. No one can see it. It's quite dark outside. So, for all of the self-identified females, it is a leap of faith.

Regrettably, faith is not rewarded in this world. Randy as Tosca as Oprah tries to convince her remaining houseguests that all that moaning and gnashing of teeth in the night air is some kind of illusion. Oprah would never mislead the sisterhood. To prove the point, Randy as Tosca as Oprah will jump last and close the circle. Worst case scenario, she survives because many before her make the ultimate sacrifice to break her fall. No, the ultimate sacrifice is not the *leap*, per se, so much as *belief* in the leap.

Effectively, Randy as Tosca as Oprah almost re-victimizes herself, framing suicide with a treacherous piece of honesty from the original production, "Vissi d'arte" ("I lived for art"). But no sooner has she spoken than Randy as Tosca as Oprah steps back from the precipice and swells to the role of witness to the carnage. Indeed, condo lights go on like a Christmas tree and first responders ignite a siren for every broken siren on the courtyard parquet. It turns out that gross economic surplus for some is not economic justice for all. Is that *really* what *A Night at the Oprah [sic]* was all about? Well, Randy as Tosca as Oprah isn't risking her navy midi dress by Atelier Versace to find out. That particular garment belongs to *A Wrinkle in Time* or fantasy fiction for children.

Dakhma

Pooja's guests didn't like her because she was strange and outward, *strange* because she made incomprehensible decisions and *outward* because she wasn't shy about making them. Certainly, Pooja's party was a case in point. No one in her right mind would serve *puran poli*, flatbread stuffed with sweet lentil, followed by *modak*, sweet flour dumplings stuffed with coconut, nutmeg and saffron. As a midday snack, it was all too much!

But there was no criticizing Pooja to her face. Her dead husband's money had indentured each and every one of them. Indrani's children enjoyed a private school education thanks to Sunjoy. Punita's foundation – *Green Mumbai* - was also financed by Sunjoy. Tanvi and Bhagyashree worked at the university whose business wing was paid for by Sunjoy. And Kanika was a publisher who had printed Sunjoy's execrable love poetry in exchange for legacy gifts. These miserable facts produced self-mockery with colonial roots: "Oh, but we must curry favour!"

Said Indrani, Pooja's sister, "How can you be depressed in a house like that? Impossible!"

Said Tanvi, the fundraiser, "She says those stupid stuffed animals help her with depression. What, she can't afford pistachio and almonds?"

Punita, the activist, said, "And did you see that sinister thing she cradles like a baby?"

Bhagyashree, professor of psychology and communication, said, "That *sinister thing* is her depression doll. She carries it around with her like an oxygen tank and a victim card."

"Methinks," said Kanika, "the lady doth protest too much."

No one could trump much less explain Kanika's use of Shakespeare. Punita put everyone out of her misery and used one word as a trampoline. "*Protest*? Did you see how she poo-pooed my menstrual advice?"

Bhagyashree said, "When she talks, her arms flap like a bird's wings. That's a very superficial person!"

Kanika added, ironically as it were, "No one's dying in a home like that!" Of course, she and the others fell silent. Pooja's husband had, indeed, died in that very home for unpublished reasons.

As the blood relative, it was Indrani's job to forgive insensitive comments by adding to the effluent. "I would have married that old fart to live in Malabar Hill!"

"And," said Kanika, lifting her goodie bag for evidence, "we all come away with these worthless trinkets. She needs the money?" No one was forgiving Kanika's second stupid comment. The party wasn't a pyramid scheme. The *trinkets* were gifts.

Punita walked back the conversation. "Can you imagine being mounted by that loathsome, hairy creature?"

The question was disingenuous. Everyone, including the speaker, knew more than one thing about Sunjoy's generous endowments.

In any event, the silence reverberated deeply in the well of Punita's self-concept. She regretted her own prurient silliness and replaced disgust for the *loathsome hairy creature* with respect for his corpse: "He deserved a better fate than to become food for the birds."

No one was aware of Punita's crisis. They were still processing memories of sex with Pooja's dead husband. To what degree does a woman's lot change when each and every penis is a prosecutor with a long list of questions seeking favourable reply?

Finally, someone brayed like a goat. All laughed.

Earlier that day, when all her guests had taken seats, Pooja explained the reason for her party. "I have fallen in love with Moomins." And she brought out what appeared to be stuffed, white hippopotamuses with names like Moominmamma and Moominpappa and Moomintroll and Sniff and Snork and Stinky. Said Pooja, "They have been a great comfort to me since Sunjoy's passing."

All of Pooja's guests looked at each other in stunned abeyance and thought more or less the same thing: *How strange and outward*!

Pooja hugged the Moomin family and hangers-on and explained that they were a fun and adventurous group with a huge following that circled the globe. "It's no secret," she said, "that I suffer from depression. All the Moomin stories have philosophy and morals." She retreated to the kitchen to retrieve tea in Moomin porcelain cups.

In the interim, everyone circulated books stored beneath the coffee table. One was a copy of the Karma Sutra whose dog-eared pages identified sexual positions and the others were chapbooks of love poetry all written by Sunjoy and dedicated to *the only woman I have ever loved*. Each of the guests believed the dedication a kind of riddle directed at her. But Kanika, the publisher, was particularly embarrassed when Bhagyashree read a random line, "*The goddess of love and desire sits/on your stomach and I enter/her temple to worship.*"

Indrani changed the subject by returning to an old theme, "How can she be depressed in a house like this? She certainly doesn't look any worse for wear."

And Tanvi whispered, "She says these stupid stuffed animals help her with depression. Would it kill her to serve a pistachio or an almond?"

Regrettably, after tea was served, Pooja was wrong-footed in her attempt to explain a Moomin cartoon. Firstly, her guests appeared to be breaking a fast of some sort. Each swallowed the puran poli and the modak like a mongoose a serpent. Secondly, Punita, the activist, appeared to be conducting a feminine hygiene seminar simultaneous to Pooja's recounting of a Moomin tale.

Said Pooja, "Moominpappa goes camping."

Punita said, "Sanitary pads made of bamboo travel well."

Pooja said, "Moominmamma packs a lunch."

Punita said, "Period-proof underwear is best when the flow is lighter."

Pooja said, "Moomintroll stays home. He confronts Groke, a mysterious grey shadow."

Punita said, "Some use tampons made of organic cotton with biodegradable cardboard applicators."

Pooja said, "Moomintroll and Groke embrace as friends."

Punita said, "I personally prefer a menstrual cup made of medical-grade silicone. It's time to reduce our ecological footprint!"

Indrani, housekeeper at the Taj Mahal Palace, said, "Well, the only ecological footprints I see are body fluids. Those tourists aren't monks and nuns. Or," she added, "maybe they are!"

Pooja, for some reason, burst into tears at the same time that her guests burst into laughter. Consequently, she corralled Groke under one arm and ran into the kitchen.

Indrani said, shaking her head, "She's always been too emotional."

Said Bhagyashree, the expert in communications, "Her arms move all over the place when she tells a story."

Indrani said, "And so like a child! Sunjoy leaves her a fortune and she replaces him with plush toys and a depression doll!"

Tanvi said, "She's a real hand talker, that one!"

Punita said, "I think a menstrual cup is more important than stuffed hippopotamuses!"

Kanika said, "It's like being inches from an airplane propeller!"

"Or," said Tanvi, "the conductor of an orchestra!"

Indrani said, "Even as a girl, if you tied up her wrists, she was mute as a gourd."

Bhagyashree nodded and concluded gravely, "Her narration of a story is point to point and gesture to gesture. She draws things in the air. She doesn't understand philosophy or morals. You have to keep your hands at your side for that."

Kanika said, "The best poets don't talk with their hands."

Tanvi said, "Unless they're making love!"

All the guests laughed and passed around photo albums of Pooja, Sunjoy and their grown children. The talking point was the straight, white teeth of Azad, Zain and Kiara, how the smile of each had the strength of a thousand suns.

Said Indrani, "No one can be depressed if your children enjoy that kind of dental work."

"Surely," said Tanvi, "they could crack an almond or a pistachio with teeth like that!"

Pooja reappeared from the kitchen and silenced the laughter with a grave announcement, "Groke and I are going to pay our respects to Sunjoy." The Moomin doll called Groke had a hill-shaped body with two cold staring eyes and a wide row of white shiny teeth.

Pooja's request was understood and uncontested. She was the executor of Sunjoy's fortune and held the purse strings. No one dared make an excuse.

In any event, *paying respects* meant hiking through the *doongerwadi* or the massive garden on the hill north of the pool and tennis courts. Everyone followed Pooja at a distance that was simultaneously respectful and disrespectful.

Said Tanvi, the fundraiser, "This forest could be sold off for a fortune!"

Said Kanika, the publisher of poetry, "I don't like not knowing where I'm going."

Said Indrani, the scrubber of surfaces, "Did you see the teeth on that Groke doll? Pooja's children have the same creepy smile!"

Said Bhagyashree, the psychologist, "It's a kind of adjustment disorder."

At that point, the air became foul.

Indrani whispered, "What stinks?"

Bhagyashree said, "You smell it, too?"

Tanvi said, "Whatever that stink is, even our prime minister couldn't sell it!"

The guests followed their noses and Pooja until they came to a large, roofless structure with only one iron door and eighteen foot walls. Said Pooja, "My husband was a Parsi. He was granted burial rites here. This place is called a *dakhma* or tower of silence. The Parsis dispose of the dead body by exposing it to the appetite of vultures. I cannot," she said, "be buried with my husband. This fact depresses me."

But Pooja was wrong-footed in her attempt to explain the rest of the ritual. Her own exposition produced another competing story from Punita, the activist.

Said Pooja, "The soul's cosmic transition is aided by the vulture's mystic eye and the feeding of one's dead body to the birds is considered an act of charity"

Punita said, "A hundred thousand flamingoes came to Mumbai this year."

Pooja countered, "Many vultures have died. They ate bovine carcasses infected with a toxic drug. Their livers failed."

Punita said, "The flamingoes are more pollution tolerant than vultures. They feed on the blue green algae from organic sewage in wetlands."

Pooja said, "Their habitat was taken."

"Not so with the flamingoes," said Punita. "Many feed in the Seawoods wetland."

Screamed Tanvi, "That's near here!"

Said Kanika, "They're absolutely gorgeous! I've seen them on television!"

Indrani said, "Tourists flock to the hotel to go see the flamingos!"

"It's disgusting," said Punita. "They have the ecological footprints of giants! They're worse than vultures!"

Pooja said, "It used to take a day. Now, consumption of the body often takes weeks. There are too few vultures."

Kanika said, "What? Who's got the biggest footprint? The tourists or the flamingoes?"

"I watched," said Pooja, "as small numbers of vultures swooped in and out daily. Some removed themselves with strips of my husband's flesh still hanging from their beaks and claws."

Pooja's guests fell silent. Each tried to reconcile the rotting buffet of Sunjoy's corpse with the wealthy Indian of singular endowments that each had known in the biblical sense, sometimes repeatedly. And it was no small morbidity, Sunjoy's putrescence and Pooja's prolonged spectatorship.

In any event, their hostess continued: "Putrefying matter is washed out by the rains and into wells of sand and charcoal well beyond the tower of silence."

Punita spoke without thinking. "Where," she said, "it is possible to imagine, these liquefied remains find underground channels to the feeding grounds of the flamingoes."

Everyone fell silent again. Had Sunjoy's *liquid remains* leeched into the Seaweeds wetland and become food for the flamingoes? Were flamingoes and vultures interchangeable predators? And how would Pooja react to the news?

In fact, Pooja's expression was that of an illusionist at the reveal moment of her card trick. "Groke and I," she said, smiling with satisfaction, "are going to see the flamingoes." She added, to make her point clear, "We will pay our respects to Sunjoy."

But her point was not clear. Pooja was using the majestic plural to refer to herself and Groke, her mysterious grey shadow. The guests complained that they were neither equipped nor dressed for the beach. Said Pooja, clarifying her intentions, "You can all find your automobiles in the carpark. Gifts are in the portico. Goodbye."

Pooja's guests were grateful that Pooja's last word was *goodbye*. It would have been uncomfortable to accompany her.

Later that afternoon, Pooja and Groke stood at the perimeter of a walking tour led by the Konkan Wetland Grievance Redressal Committee. One man used his arms to indicate a great expanse of water and fowl. Said the man, "Authorities at the Industrial Development Corporation call this a *depression* and not a *lake*. They hope to defeat us with the magical use of language. *A lake has rights*, they say. *We can do nothing for a depression*."

While the man continued his narrative, describing the dumping of industrial debris and organic sewage, his listeners began to drown his text with *oohs* and *aahs*. Indeed, a massive flock of flamingoes had blotted the sun and were extending landing gear.

When the furor had subsided, the man refurbished his speech to address new realities on the ground. "They always stay together. They are an extremely gregarious species." The group followed the pointer finger of the group leader and absorbed hundreds of flamingos bobbing in the murky green water. "They have sewage to thank for their food supply. The phenomenon is called Edge Nature. You see what we're up against," he said, "a vulnerable lake, toxic effluent and an explosion of elegant pink birds. The worst emergency is the one you can't see."

Pooja and Groke were left alone when the group proceeded further south to observe the destruction of catchment areas.

To an objective eye, this last decision was strange and outward. Pooja removed her *shalwar kameez*, a long sleeveless tunic and pleated trousers held up with an elastic belt. She was not wearing underwear.

She began to wade into the Seaweeds depression with Groke firmly underarm. As she narrowed the distance between herself and the flamingoes, she navigated the kinds of weeds that draw blood and raise welts. She did not know that her foot had compressed beneath her a silicone, menstrual cup.

Where the depth of the depression was greatest, Pooja began to cycle her legs through the flamboyance of flamingoes. She had already made the decision not to use her arms when she *paid her respects*, so much more so because Bhagyashree had said, *She doesn't understand philosophy or morals. You have to keep your hands at your side for that.*

Perhaps Pooja believed she was taking her place with Sunjoy among the DNA of the world and that hers was an act of charity. In any event, her last waking memories were crimson or black tipped bills and low gabbling and growling sounds. Thereafter, Pooja's mysterious grey shadow popped its head above the surface of the water and turned its cold staring eyes and white shiny teeth toward the exodus of the pink sky and the tower of silence that tumbled in its wake.

Dementia

He remembers the tree shaker machine, the cricket whir of hydraulics, shock waves through the compression arm, the smell of diesel, the percolating bubble of leaves and nuts that strike with the fury of locusts and the ground-sewn nets to lasso the harvest. "I remember," he says.

But she does, too: the *YouTube* video they watched years later – *Tree Shaker Destructor*. What the two of them *actually* saw, what she narrates *in painstaking detail…* the *campesinos* collect the almonds in burlap pouches, tap the small branches with field hockey sticks from the local *colegio concertado* and produce small, shrinking batches of nut diaspora. How does he *do* that, she wonders, remember what *wasn't* so sensually, consign to the ash heap what *was*?

Three months later, Ian's wound opening like an evil flower, he says something obscene to settle the score, counterpunches cruelty for embarrassment, "Your best friend, Evelyn, that lived on Frederica Street in Westfort…" And he immediately conjures pornographic locutions to describe what they did, (in perfect parallel structure – rutting, contorting, licking), how he never gave her the *real skinny* on any of this because they did it like animals and animals don't talk.

Of course, Catherine believes none of it. She's been through all the caregiver seminars, taken all her vaccinations, so to speak, knows that Ian resents her perfect recollections of the past, (*corrections* she makes mostly by accident, sometimes to punish him for his illness). And when Ian embellishes, *silly boy*, she has to smile. Apparently, he and Evelyn enjoyed their sexual trysts in Spain between stages of *La Vuelta a España*. Ian would rack his bike and then rack Evelyn. *Evelyn*, she who never left Thunder Bay, she whose idea of trespass is to willfully mix up the recycling. And then he says, tongue in serpent cheek, "That was the time the locals collected almonds in gardener sacks."

Catherine touches Ian's grey hair with absolute tenderness. *Well played, my world class cyclist, my almond eater, my angry apostate from the church of love.*

And love they did, the kind of love that produces itself magically, like pack film from an old Polaroid camera: (now, Catherine knows, Ian would make a hash of it, pull/tear at odd angles, have developer goo all over his hands, mistime the exposure). But their first meeting in Thunder Bay was sixty, sticky seconds to change the world. She and her parents finish ice cream and arrive at Kakabeka Falls in dad's ancient Chevy Impala, disgorge into crisp spring air that bores Catherine, she who can think of nothing else but starting her English studies at the University of Toronto.

The parking lot is big enough for a rodeo but the cyclist overtakes her at arm's length, startles her, creates a slipstream she will never leave, cooperative, commensal, exhilarating (until the onset of the disease makes everything more tactical and competitive, saps her, okay, *their* energy).

"Hey!" she says, admiring his butt in spandex, not knowing what to make of the curly, brown tufts of hair escaping his helmet like thistle through concrete rifts.

"Sorry," he says, stopping, turning.

Now, she's winded, too, like air brakes bled of air.

"So, you're a cyclist?"

He's not immune to sexual attraction, whatever else is happening here, tries to stretch his field of vision to include her eyes and her short shorts.

"Yeah," he says, "I hope to be in the *Tour de France* one day."

Catherine, wildly impetuous, rushes to the car at conversation's end, locates a pencil, tears a strip from the sleeve of her sugar cone.

He says, stuffing her phone number into his fanny pack, "I've still got half a country to cover. I'll call you when I finish."

The rest of the afternoon, while walking, she feels like she's pedalling furiously on a stationary bike. As they always do, mom and dad name and annotate geography and history: the Kaministiquia River, the Precambrian Shield, glaciers and meltwater. The only thing that resonates with Catherine is dad's last contribution, "The name Kakabeka comes from the Ojibwe word *gakaabikaa,* meaning, *waterfall over a cliff.*"

Catherine, panting, "Oh, my God, *yes.*"

If that was the moment of conception, then the *other* beginning, the beginning of the end, was surely their consultation with Dr. Singh at Toronto Western Hospital. Ian discovers he has Alzheimer's disease. The diagnosis is not *completely* unexpected but only in the way you predict your own death. It *looks* inevitable, but you're still hoping for another one or thirty good years.

According to the literature, Ian isn't supposed to deny his feelings, but this is common currency with him. Virile, generous-hearted Ian will admit no toxicity. Whatever the apocalypse, he maintains his orbit around Catherine, like a satellite with a death ray for whomever or whatever might sully their love affair. This time, in fact, he outdoes himself.

To Doctor Singh, he says, "I don't want it."

"Sorry?"

"I don't want *his* disease."

The doctor says nothing, her brow pinched with confusion. Catherine, the English professor, remembers the grammar lesson for Ian, the kinesiologist.

What, exactly, does an apostrophe do?

Assign ownership of something to someone.

Catherine, to Doctor Singh, "It's *Alzheimer's* disease. It belongs to *him*. He can keep it."

Ian and Catherine squeeze each other's hand for confirmation of their clever *pas de deux*. Smiles of love and forbearance develop the theme, are protective ozone, an immune response to the wound. *Real reckoning will come later and very soon.*

Dr. Singh sees no humor in punctuation. Fair enough. Ian asks to speak to her privately. *Typical*. Catherine acquiesces, for her own sake.

Indeed, reckoning arrives for Catherine in the time it takes to slide her weight against the wall in the hallway. It feels exactly like that time she lost consciousness from sunstroke and keeled over, arms flailing while her legs are cut out from under her. The tears converge mightily: rain, eavestroughs, gravity. Catherine's hand won't stop them. Certainly, her arm won't. *Well, this is a shitty turn of events.* The self-talk is a distancing device. The speaker doesn't even sound like her, but that's the idea. *Jesus, Ian, what are we going to do?* Oh, boy, there's another hazard in the water, what she said after discovering she couldn't have children (sad/glad many times since), what she *will* say, sort of, in the last stage of Ian's sickness when his *personal care* is no longer a saccharine euphemism. *Jesus, Ian, what am I going to do?*

By the time Ian surfaces, invites Catherine to return with him into Doctor Singh's office, she has been busking grief for fifteen minutes, regaling passers-by with sobbing, convulsing and auto-asphyxia; in atmospheric terms, a *rain event*, a one in one hundred year's storm, which is about right for the weather, but Catherine knows she should expect a hundred more of these centennial events.

Ian doesn't even say good-bye to Doctor Singh. He takes Catherine's mortified body into his arms. She can't verbalize it, can't even *think* the words, but she knows this is all wrong: *who has the disease that belongs to Alzheimer? Who?*

And this won't be her first misstep. Turns out, they're *all* her missteps. They were in Spain, again. She was *sure* of it. There was a huge accident during one of the speed stages of the race. Ian insists the accident took place during an event in Thunder Bay, on the bike path around Boulevard Lake. He is so childlike, so petulant. "No, no, no," he parrots. "*You're wrong*. It was in Thunder Bay!" The realization overtakes her slowly, fearfully, like the eye of a lizard calibrated to open by millimetre. How is that possible? *How?* She remembers the disturbing gaggle of cycler limbs and bicycle chrome *on the bike path around Boulevard Lake.* Ian narrowly escaped injury, saved himself for *this*. The next day, he would describe the trauma scene, the ugliness of it, as a scrambled brain. *He* said it. She didn't.

All she can think now, as her eyes water, *forgive me.*

And she creeps into her bedroom, like a dead thing or a battered woman. She lays herself delicately on her bed, compresses beneath her weight the piles of student papers she has neatly arranged there. Each is an essay on a familiar tome that she has taught for years – *By Grand Central Station I Lay Down and Wept*. If she were alert to anything at all beyond suffering, she might see the neat parallel between the novel's protagonist and herself, how they are betrayed and exiled from love, how Ian has taken an octopus brain to be his consort, all mimicry, reflexive intimidation and inky camouflage – hidden from his wife and his own better nature. But she's only alert to their love as a vacuum bomb, an aerosol cloud of speeding shrapnel that easily penetrates erstwhile conduits of memory and hope.

To see it any other way would be *dementia*.

(Hogtied Girl)

P. Y. Preston Street is a mixed residential neighbourhood full of Chamber of Commerce suits, school teachers, retirees, drug dealers and welfare cheats. It was a strange sight, a boy walking down P. Y. Preston Street with a Zebco Predator spincast and a Ziploc container full of mulching worms. Everything about it was 1950's Americana, the *Beaver* tethered by love to June and Ward Cleaver. Conversely, if Jake was from the near future, he might have had a mobile phone and an AR app for Pokémon Go. He might have walked into a tree. Game over. No Predator. No predation.

In hindsight, I imagine one or more of the people watching my brother was a pedophile. I did my homework after what happened. On average, the neighbourhood's got at least one sex offender on every block. If you want, you can see the profiles of pedophiles pop up on your computer screen as you move your cursor. Maybe pedophiles see victims as pop-ups, too, three-dimensional objects that surge upward from the pages of a children's book. The pedophile's goal is to activate the tab that drops the victim's underwear.

Jake was ten years old when he hatched the idea of landing a whopper. According to the law, you can be on your own at that age. It's a judgement call. Even so, mom and dad had appointed me *in loco parentis* for the afternoon, that five-minute-away, responsible person whose symbolic value is reassuring and whose practical value, in the event of an actual emergency, is diddly-squat. No one says it, but we all know it's true.

Case in point, by supper time, Jake was still not home. I'm sure my parents had already started to *remote view* sundry grim scenarios. There was an air pressure change to go with the declining light outside. Nonetheless, they continued to work furiously at the sand castle before the encroaching tide. My mom, one to worry more, assured my dad that all was well. I, myself, was watching *The Young and the Restless* on T.V. and, phone in hand, scrolling through a backlog of tweets from Kanye West. Whatever mom and dad were saying was buck up self-talk, heavily redacted, emergency ticker at the bottom of my television screen.

I don't know why we didn't take the car. Maybe our walking toward the river by way of P. Y. Preston Street was an obvious sign of our dithering and anxiety or maybe we walked to normalize our actions, to convince ourselves that haste was unnecessary and inelegant or maybe we walked because we were in no hurry to see the sum of our fears.

In any event, the sum of my parents' fears was the kind of math that left you feeling like cut bait. Jake looked like a calf in a rodeo, that event where the terror-stricken beast is lassoed, tossed to the ground and hogtied. He was motionless, his pants and underwear around his ankles. The shape of his small body was that of a question mark. His eyes were closed and he appeared to be unconscious or dead. His worm container was upended, worms making snotty geometry on flat grey rock.

My brother was breathing, but he had a gash on his head. Mom yanked up his pants and his underwear and dad carried him home. On the way to the hospital, Jake came to, of sorts. He moaned and his pupils moved behind his eyelids, like he was watching a movie. I hoped the movie was entertaining, perhaps the best he could hope for, when all else was dark.

This is where things metastasize into other things equally sinister and shocking. The nurse at the intake desk asked for details about the *accident*. Jake would see a doctor immediately. He was prone on a gurney and already being whisked away. Mom and dad looked at each other and colluded in a heartbeat, began to build the story outward. How did they arrive there so quickly, so ingenuously? Was it a yellow brick road or a hot air balloon? "He went down to Neebing River -" "to fish for smelt." "He must have fallen -" "and hit his head." "He was playing -" "a game on the rocks." "He fell and hit his head." *Whopper*.

Discussion for the next few days was all about concussion protocol. The train pulling evidence preservation, police and crisis centre was switched to the end of a very flat earth. Conveniently, Jake remembered nothing of his *accident*, was groggy and headachy for many days in his dark, shuttered bedroom. *Sensitive to light*, I was told.

Weeks later, he defended himself through a poker face that hid everything or nothing, "Asking me over and over again what I remember doesn't change what I remember. What do you want me to remember? Just say it and I'll remember it for you." I think, *Are you telling tales out of school?*

Speaking of mom and dad, I tried to spit the bit out of my mouth, communicate sadness, outrage, the cost of my own complicity, anything beyond judgment suspended in the wind. Before I could open a dialogue, dad interrupts me, floats another whopper, "We won't blame you if you talk about what you think you saw." *Think I saw?* Upping the ante, mom tries to stitch my lips wide shut, bundle a confidence and a threat, "Say what you believe. We'll tell everyone it's not your fault. We'll make certain your brother understands it's not your fault. You were watching *The Young and the Restless*. You were reading tweets from Kanye West."

June and Ward Cleaver were giving me the sharp and sharper edges of a psychological wedge. Shut up and suffer. Talk and suffer much more. It was diabolical. It was predictable. Most parents will do anything to save their sons, including repurposing the ashes of their daughters. No one says it, but we all know it's true.

It's not your fault. It's not your fault. It's not your fault.
Hogtied.

The Brief, Sad Tale of Ping Pong

    Varunthip adopted a four-legged friend to replace the grandchild that her own child refused to provide. Three days later, Ping Pong lost one of those legs in an automobile accident. Before the dog could bleed out, Varunthip used the membrane of one hundred chicken eggs to treat the wound. As a result, her husband, Theewarat, ate *Kai Loog Keui* (Son-in-Law Eggs) for a period of four weeks. In the event that Ping Pong suffer a second dismemberment, Theewarat asked his wife to treat the wound with the leaves of the Woolly Lamb's Ear. He would never eat eggs, again.
    At least, that's what he said. Varunthip caught her husband eating *Poi Thong* (Golden Egg Yolk Threads) with Seoul Joe, a neighbour who had fought in the Korean War to preserve democracy and, later, his inalienable right to stream porn. Varunthip said to her husband, "You don't hate eggs. You hate Ping Pong." Theewarat lied or he spoke truth to power. There was no middle ground. "Wife," he said, "your dog is a curse. He should be thrown out with the trash." And then he explained, in so many words, that it had nothing to do with ableism.
    Effectively, Varunthip and Theewarat had been shunned since the day of Ping Pong's accident. Villagers believed them a source of bad luck and averted their eyes and kept a distance of at least nine feet. Many wore amulets depicting a meditating Buddha juxtaposed with a giant cobra sporting large breasts and a negligee. Theewarat's nuclear option (one dog brain/one human bullet) was never considered. Villagers feared the return of Ping Pong as a ghost as much as they feared the spirit world of dead children.
    Ironically enough, forestalling the ghostly return of a dead baby restored Ping Pong's reputation as did the answer to a playful question: what do a cat and a three-legged dog have in common? *How each shits* was the answer. Since his accident, Ping Pong had adopted the feline habit of digging a hole for his poop and meticulously covering it afterward. Varunthip said that Ping Pong communicated with the spirit world by licking his phantom limb and burying his own scat. Theewarat, who had learned English by watching pornography with Seoul Joe, said that Ping Pong was simply a *pussy* for refusing to challenge more dominant dogs.

In any event, Varunthip let the animal out at midnight to do his business. Ping Pong limped through a torrential downpour toward the cassava field whose fertilizer was one inch of human excrement. After that, the beginning of the story is more legend than fact. Ping Pong did not smell afterbirth in the sand and shit, as some said, nor did he dig a hole for his poop, as most said. Rather, the rains exposed the tops of tubers and the soft crown of one particular baby's head. At this point, Ping Pong latched onto the infant's umbilical cord and dragged it into the home. No one was any wiser until the dog's tongue excavated mud from the baby's mouth.

Varunthip wanted to keep the child because she was sick and tired of waiting for Phatcharakorn, her own daughter, to give her grandchildren. "The baby," she said, "belongs to us. It grew in our cassava field. Ping Pong's harvest has answered my prayers." Because he spoke porn English, Theewarat responded to this and a knock at the door with irony both intended and unintended, "Your harvest story has come a crapper."

Effectively, police had already arrested the baby's teen mother who had managed to hide from her parents the bump beneath her LeBron James jersey. Varunthip was compelled to clean the infant with a garden hose and hand it over to child services. She also had to remove one of Ping Pong's spare collars and a tunic of cassava sack cloth. As a parting gesture, Varunthip cautioned those receiving the infant to beware of its grandmother who was clearly indolent and, like the baby, soft in the head.

Afterward, this trebled the animosity that she felt toward Phatcharakorn whose *western ideas* included waiting for Mr. Right. She blamed herself because she had once called her own baby *cute* instead of *ugly* and attracted jealous spirits who poisoned her daughter's libido and dried up in her *the organs of increase*. As a result, she asked her husband to whittle an erect penis from teakwood. Surely, frigidity was no match for prayer and a penis icon or, failing that, a LeBron James jersey. Theewarat said he would take on the project but, of course, he would have to carve from distant memory.

In any event, Ping Pong's reputation turned the corner abruptly. The three-legged monstrosity of bad luck had become a three-legged emissary of windfall blessings. And no one was more invested, literally, than Theewarat, the unbeliever. In front of the family home, he set up a kiosk of all things *Ping Pong* for which villagers were only too happy to pay or barter. Chief among the wares on display were Ping Pong's urine, scat and hair.

Business was brisk. Neighbours believed one or more of these things would bring good luck at the races, an advantageous interest rate at the bank or help with making speeches. Varunthip knew her husband was a cynical profiteer but she did not dislike stockpiles of baby formula or kerosene. She also sought to profit from Ping Pong's other-worldly powers, dunking a picture of her daughter in the dog's urine in order to boost the girl's sex drive.

It was a shock to everyone when Ping Pong died. He vomited an undigested eel, rolled onto his back and gave up the ghost. So angry was Varunthip that she pummelled the eel with a granite pestle until the creature disgorged a thousand eggs. After that, there were only two things left to do: plan a funeral and create the conditions of a bubble nest within an empty pickle jar. Into this soupy mixture of egg and reed, Varunthip would routinely dip a photo of Phatcharakorn while praying to Dewi Sri, the Indonesian goddess of rice and fertility. "My daughter will have a daughter," she predicted, "and we will call her, Jasmine."

Everyone knew when Phatcharakorn had returned home because she spoke little but sang often and sadly like a bird in a shrinking forest. Varunthip got out of bed and pursued her daughter's sonorous melancholy. Said Phatcharakorn, "I have come to help you grieve." "You know," said her mother, "those who sing in the kitchen are doomed to have an old boyfriend or none at all." Phatcharakorn replied, immodestly for her, "You must remove that vanity mirror from your bedroom. You obsess over sex." Theewarat wasn't so sure. He entered the kitchen with an announcement of his own, "She's made a monk out of me."

The plan was to go to the Wat Krathum Suea Pla temple in Bangkok. Real monks were performing real funeral rites for dogs, cats, elephants and horses. Varunthip told Theewarat that she believed in the *samsara* life and death cycle and potential reincarnation. She also told Theewarat that Ping Pong would return as a swarthy human male who would sweep Phatcharakorn off her feet and impregnate her shriven body with human sperm and eel egg in magical cohort. She gave the whole process twenty-four hours. In any event, the ceremony, itself, would cost 3,000 *baht* or roughly the amount earned by Theewarat selling Ping Pong indulgences of hair, shit and urine. Theewarat was not amused. He said, "She'll ball a guy when she's ready."

    The dog's body was packed in ice in a Coca Cola cooler and loaded onto a long-tail boat in the Mekong. The boat was propelled by a truck engine mounted on an inboard pole. It was important to get to the hotel before midnight because, said Varunthip, they would be charged two days if they booked one and arrived the next. In any event, she and Phatcharakorn sat cross-legged in the backdraft of diesel fuel. Varunthip haggled with the ship's navigator for a better spot, but, she was told, Ping Pong and the cooler constituted *cartage*. For a little more money, the women could move forward without their cooler. Of course, Varunthip would hear none of it. She would stay at Ping Pong's side until his remains had served their purpose.

    The long-tail boat navigated a series of *klongs* or canals as it neared the hotel near the Buddhist temple where Ping Pong would receive last rites. At one point, the boat entered a floating market flooded with tourists. Varunthip purchased helmet crab egg salad from a vendor in a paddle dinghy. Phatcharakorn did not eat, but she did buy feed for fishes. Effectively, she stared intensely at hundreds of huge catfish swarming the waters and she, like the tourists, launched handfuls of colourful food pellets. She heard a tour operator bark through a megaphone, "They taste toxic. No one eats them. And they multiply like tomorrow!" The long-boat navigator noticed her kindness and offered her the *prize* in his trouser pocket.

    Mother and daughter experienced the compression of time at journey's end. Coconut or salt farms and orchid plantations or rice fields gave way to large commercial airplanes and high-rises and exhaust from traffic, construction and burning crop stubble. Varunthip said, "Nothing's right or wrong. The cockroach or the rat or the mosquito doesn't ask if there are too many mouths to feed." Her daughter processed her mother's moral relativism as grief for her dog or commiseration for the natural world. She was a harmless old woman with old-world aspirations.

    In any event, Varunthip and Phatcharakorn disgorged into competing currents of smog and democracy. Each held either end of the Coca Cola cooler containing Ping Pong's remains and navigated direction and momentum through a pulsating and screaming crowd. Many of the demonstrators wore red shirts and white respirator masks and carried banners demanding fresh elections. Some chanted slogans against the king. Some enjoined onlookers to remember the dead from 2010. Others begged the government to give them clean air. Varunthip screamed and waved her arms impatiently, "Get out of the way!" They must, she said, arrive at the hotel by midnight or risk paying double.

Her mother pushed away the offer of a particulate mask, but Phatcharakorn did not. She tried to hook the mask around either ear with one hand, but failed. She set down the cooler, but misjudged angle and speed. Ping Pong spilled out and into the street. Protesters scooped up the hairless rigid corpse and passed it high over their heads and in a circular motion, chanting, after the fashion of one, "Give us freedom or give us death!" When Ping Pong's body had made the round, it fell into the outstretched arms of Varunthip. She quickly returned it to the cooler, spitting and screaming at the red shirts and white masks, "Bastards! Prostitutes! You'll make us late!"

They walked the remainder of the trip in silence, only stopping to switch hand grips and rest arms. A torrential rain fell, whose sound and smell recalled the night Ping Pong had disinterred a baby from a cassava patch of sand and human excrement. So intense was the darkness and the deluge that Varunthip could barely see Phatcharakorn at the other end of the cooler. Only beneath a street lamp did she notice the outline of her daughter's breasts through the wet linen of her white top. She felt vindicated and absorbed with fancy, but said nothing.

Shortly before midnight, they found their hotel on the banks of the Khlong Saen Saep. Although she would not *pay double*, Varunthip found instantly fresh provocations. She described the carpet in their room as *grubby*, the water, *grey*, the bed, *lumpy*, and the air *stinky* with barbecue and vinegar. She disappeared for a time period that was uncomfortably long, ostensibly to complain, she said. Once returned, Phatcharakorn protested her mother's fastidiousness. She wanted desperately to sleep.

But Varunthip had other ideas. She produced from her trouser pockets one neatly folded yellow jasmine flower and Theewarat's neatly whittled teakwood penis. She said to her daughter, "You must go into the garden on the hotel grounds and make an offering." She added, in a tone that was whispered and enigmatic, "You will conceive almost immediately."

Phatcharakorn did not want to argue. She was mindful of her mother's grief for the animal in the Coca Cola cooler. She understood her mother's obsession with grandchildren as the offspring of isolation and abandonment. In any event, she would return to her studies in three days and she was too exhausted to find, let alone exercise, her own free will. The corpse of Ping Pong had taken the starch out of her legs. "I'll go tomorrow morning," she said, "before the ceremony at the temple."

But her mother had other ideas. "No. You must go now. You must go at midnight." She added, "It won't work if you don't go now."

The Goddess Tubtim Shrine had hundreds of phalluses of all shapes and sizes and materials, many of which decorated with ribbons whose colors were mute in the darkness and rain. Phatcharakorn stood before the statuary as though she were an apostate in a Druid temple. In her hand, she held the teakwood penis wrapped in yellow jasmine. She already knew what she was going to do. Therefore, her own actions, like her mother's, were premeditated. She threw her offering into the bushes and released the hounds of hell.

In fact, these *hounds* recalled a scene from the movie, *The Lion King*. Perhaps it was terror and dissociation and the foreknowing of darkness. In any event, Phatcharakorn felt like a vulnerable cub surrounded by leering toothy hyenas who intended to eat her whole. She heard taunting of a particular theme through the midnight hour and the driving rain.

"Hey, baby," one said.

"Wanna baby?" said another.

"Hey, baby. Come to daddy."

Phatcharakorn counted at least five men and their hands gripped her all at once. She felt herself being pulled and elevated and her white top gone and her skirt gone and the rain and the restraint and the pneumatic weight of each as her mouth fell upon and filled with mud.

At that same moment, Varunthip tipped the Coca Cola cooler just enough to release the corpse of Ping Pong into the garbage chute. Afterward, pausing to collect her breath, she remembered the porn imagery she had once seen at Seoul Joe's, how women enjoyed double and multiple penetrations. She shook her head at the imagery and bore down on next steps. The morning would be clear of pollution and protest and foolish talk of temples and reincarnation. And – if her plan bore fruit - she would soon purchase food offerings and ankle bracelets and baby clothes with her booty of 3000 baht less, of course, the fee she had recently paid for services rendered.

The Intervention

Paul repeatedly turned the key in the ignition. The clicking of the starter was an end-stage death rattle for the battery. He tilted his head in exasperation, called his El Dorado a piece of crap. Of greater concern to John, his passenger, was the noose of sobriety around his neck. He needed gin and he needed it fast.

They got out of the car, each feeling like Noah or his wife, the world struck dead with drowning and vengeance and all the animals on board victims of starvation or anthrax. Paul tried to locate the origin of what he heard, one stroke of an internal combustion engine ricocheting between the forest and the hills and another ricocheting between his ears. He needed a drink badly.

John had the same experience of percussion and confusion. He described the two-stroke engine as possibly a chainsaw, possibly a hedge trimmer or, more likely, the throbbing of blood vessels in their heads. They were in week two of a fresh bender, one of so many that the singularity of each had almost become an infinite value. On some level, they expected to die. Maybe, they already had.

If so, the flood of despair had not killed everyone. Off to one side of the road, two crows feasted at the bottom of a dry gulch of sandy earth. Each ripped at spongy chunks of flesh and shook smaller morsels free of the larger ones. The blood splatter was carmine, rust and grey, indicating fresh and old samples.

Paul thought he recognized the spongy chunks of flesh. They reminded him of a picture he had once seen of a liver infected with cirrhosis. Maybe those livers at the side of the road grew back every day. Maybe those scrawny crows pecking at yellow wounds were penitential figures in a morality play. Each bite subtracted calories. Each bite produced wasting syndrome.

Both Paul and John stared at the polyps of flesh in the arid sand. For a moment, each thought about oozing bloody carrion on the road to oblivion. But they weren't zombies yet, even if each felt dead. They weren't interested in *brain*. They were interested in gin, rum or whiskey or, more likely in this apocalyptic setting, the distilled remains of the maguey or agave plant.

An unmarked tow-truck overtook them as they walked. Neither heard its approach. The arrival of the tow-truck was both good news and bad news. People and commerce meant liquor. Conversely, the tow-truck was pulling Paul's El Dorado. John wondered if the driver was a humanitarian or a scavenger. Would he recharge the battery or sell the car for scrap? Paul waxed poetic. He said the crows and the tow-truck would lead each of them toward the kingdom of spirits. He dreamed liquor, not supernatural beings.

It turned out that salvation was man's best friend. A small dog appeared from around a bend in the road. He looked to be a Xolo, a grey miniature. Anyway, he would advance, stop and canter backwards, advance and retreat. Paul and John read greater evidence for pursuit of the lumpy hills. Collectively, black crows, an unmarked tow-truck and a Mexican hairless dog spelled *booze*. This all seemed perfectly reasonable conjecture.

The first house they saw was a California bungalow. John vaguely recognized the full-width porch supported by stone columns. And he vaguely recognized the low-slung roof with wide eaves. The wide eaves reminded him of the time he had been too sick to dislodge the leaf litter, how a rainstorm had overwhelmed the clogged gutter and produced undulating waves of water on an interior wall. His wife had complained that he was useless or careless or something *less* than he should be. John described the damage to their home as bad luck or an act of God.

Anyway, this day was hot and he unbuttoned his shirt to release humidity. He tried to look inside the home, but the windows were opaque, like his own eyes. He couldn't see anything inside, but he could hear celebration out back - voices, laughter, a familiar retro party mix and, most importantly, the clinking of glasses.

The banner at the barbecue announced the fortieth birthday of his ex-wife. Laura greeted him with a cola and a hotdog and a look of apprehension. The food and soda vibrated in John's hands and made him feel sick. He said he couldn't stay, because he hadn't come in the first place. Way back when, he had forgotten that day the same way folk forget things when their thoughts are elsewhere. John liked to say he was only human.

The dog pulled them further on down the road toward a high school. Paul parked one hand in his long, shaggy beard and peered quizzically at the structure. He could not place a memory, but the fight to locate one competed with a murderous desire for alcohol. That was it. The memory of high school and the hot humid day produced an overwhelming need for refreshment.

Suddenly, students spilled out the front door and onto the front steps. A band played *The Graduation March* and teachers formed a receiving line. At the bottom of the steps, all the students launched academic caps into the air, laughed and embraced. Parents jockeyed for pictures and waved at their children.

Paul recognized his daughter, Sarah. His daughter looked at him with great pity and love. She gestured for him to approach, but Paul couldn't stay because he hadn't come, anyway. That day was a blur. He thinks he was in someone's garage or basement or shed. He thinks he was cheering someone up, but he can't remember who or why. In a similar way, he vaguely remembers misplacing his visitation rights, like he did blocks of hours and days on the calendar. He admits to himself great confusion. Paul would be the first to say he wasn't perfect.

But neither Paul nor John was confused about Sam. The dog galloped toward and stopped in front of a ranch house with a long low profile and large windows. Sam was replacing damaged cedar boards in a sundeck and the new guys were laying mulch around firebush shrubs. Two small signs dotted the front lawn and announced Sam's home improvement and landscaping business.

Paul and John hated Sam with a passion. Each saved and invented special language for Sam, language that was righteous and degrading. It was Sam who had fired them more than once for a variety of phantom offenses. Apparently, feeling poorly was actionable. Not coming to work because you were feeling poorly was reason enough for termination. Each man raised a middle finger in the direction of Sam's back. Each invited him to become a compass needle on that finger.

The dog was now stopped before a cemetery. He spun like a whirling dervish in one direction and then the other. Like the tall overcast day, the dog appeared to lack direction before the rows upon rows of dead souls. He struck a pose that reflected the awful surprise of cardiac arrest. And then he threw himself onto his side, his legs simulating rigor mortis and his eyes rolled backward. It would be the last time Paul or John would see the Mexican hairless, his mock death a kind of Homeric simile.

Their own respectful relationship with death had begun as a dare. In fact, their first meeting had been at a house party when each was an adolescent. At evening's end, they were asked to drain all remaining glasses of their dregs. Paul and John became known for that, finishing the drinks of others at party's end. Over time, a dissolute caper became a sacred ceremony. Everyone cheered, clapped and enjoyed the feeling of vindication.

But, in this case, the amber afterglow of high school hijinks produced only ash. Each drank lustily from the cups left at the grave sites. Each spat the beverage immediately, a *champurrado* of chocolate, corn flour, milk and anise seed. Paul vomited while John's chest heaved without result. Neither noticed that the tombstones read, respectively, *Pablo* and *Juan*.

It was a curious case of perspective. Worsening cramps and headache kept Paul and John on all fours. A pungent, sickening odor produced more retching, wet and dry. And then they were joined by an avalanche of legs and music and colorful motion that amplified their disorientation and nausea. The smell was a wet blanket of sulphur and scent gland.

It appeared to be a parade. Some wore feather headdresses and body paint depicting a skull and bones. Others wore costumes that were devil-themed. One group spun lit-up hula-hoops while marching. Others advanced on unicycles. There were giant skeletal marionettes and skeletal papier-mâché. Paul and John were literally scooped to their feet before the advance of floats and candle-covered shrines.

The grand marshal of the parade was a stilt walker dressed as a court jester. He wore a mask of bark and stiff linen that looked like a demon with goat horns. He informed Paul and John that the whole town was celebrating *el Día de los Muertos* or the Day of the Dead. It was an opportunity, he said, to commemorate friends and family who had died and to help support their spiritual journey.

Paul and John were indifferent to the festival and its purpose. Instead, they begged the grand marshal for a drink of any kind. Each said beers would be fine, anything to calm the two-stroke engine that pummelled their brains. The grand marshal produced the grin of a goat, one row of jaundiced teeth on the lower jaw. He had an explanation for the two-stroke engine.

Indeed, the machine was found at parade's end. Very large stones were inserted into the cavity between vertical, metal jaws. Compressive force created a nut-cracking motion and smaller, hand-sized pieces of stone. The toggling leavers produced an alternating beat that orbited what appeared to be an amphitheatre. The chainsaw or hedge trimmer was a rock crusher.

Paul and John surveyed the circular venue. John said he had studied one just like it in high school. It had a seating area, an arena and a *vomitorium*, broad conduits where spectators could enter or disperse quickly. John said that folk in those days would stage combats, animal slayings and executions. Paul was more interested in the topography of the amphitheatre. At the five points of a pentagram drawn in the red earth were five *cantinas*. Each had a counter or *barra* for serving patrons, but the shelves in the kiosks held no alcohol. Each of the five bars was a broken promise.

The grand marshal turned their attention toward two small curtained stages. The grand marshal said they could see one and then the other, but they couldn't look at both at the same time and they must choose. Each of the men had a sinking feeling. It had all come to this: two different ways to go with a dead battery in their El Dorado and no bars for libations and no one left to blame, but themselves.

Paul pushed through headache and cramps and nausea, said he would prefer to see the curtained stage left of their position. John was in a bad way. He said he didn't give a shit. He felt like sea kelp, awash in momentum that he could curse out but he couldn't stop, drowning but only to the point of his penultimate breath.

Paul got his wish and the scene was revealed. The faces of both men betrayed horror, sadness and shame. John vocalized the whimper of an animal, alone and starved. Paul wondered if the need for a drink hadn't produced a shared hallucination. He and John chose the contents of the second stage. One curtain closed. The other opened.

Of course, the second scene was exactly the same as the first, an act of reprisal that had long haunted their dreams. John and Paul had steeled themselves for this result. They were confronted with the illusion of choice, an endgame whose theatre was scripted and whose conclusions, for the moment, were unknown.

The stage combined the properties of playhouse and cinema, transitioned smoothly from the panelled interiors of a bungalow to a backyard vista of pool water and open air. John and Paul were teenagers. They were closing a house party with their signature devilry, draining drinks left on countertops and coffee tables. Only this time, their host joined them.

Ron was their host. He was a gap-toothed computer geek whose languages were Pascal and Fortran. Ron's parents were absent. Ron wanted entry into the illicit populism of *Johnny* and *Pauly*. Ron was drunk and agreed to a dare of his own. He would dive into the backyard pool with his clothes on.

Ron dove into the shallow end. He must have believed his wager incomplete payment for his dreams. But he would never wake up and he would never surface and he would never dream, again. He had fractured his C-4 and C-5 vertebrae and would have been paralyzed below his shoulders. Paul and John laughed, grew silent and fled.

At show's end, the grand marshal inserted the mouthpiece of a saxophone through the aperture of his mask. He produced a modified sine wave with particular vibration around the C4 and C5 positions. He wasn't *entertaining*. He was *summoning*. Paul and John cried because the circumstances of Ron's death had always been a private matter, one they had carefully curated far from the light of day. Neither could imagine escape from history. And neither could imagine escape from corrosive connections with the world.

And it might have remained that way had not the second curtain revealed a different story. The scene had been struck and rebuilt. On this stage, two adolescents were tied to the towering flower stalks of giant *maguey alto*. The thorns on the leaves of the plants were dappled in blood that was alternately carmine, rust or grey. Each of the boys was gagged and blindfolded. John and Paul watched as the costumed revelers circled the pile of stones created by the crusher. Each gathered what he could and reassembled.

The grand marshal no longer had a saxophone. The grand marshal explained to Paul and John that the adolescents had committed a heinous crime whose cumulative effect included a circular wave that had moved outward and touched and abused many. The two adolescents would be stoned to death. Paul and John were invited to participate. They heard the words *debt*, *substitution* and *atonement*.

To help with their decision-making, the men identified the key stake-holders in the drama. The amphitheatre was filling quickly with spectators. John saw his ex-wife, Laura, and Paul saw his daughter, Sarah. Their ex-boss, Sam, was there, too. Other estranged family and co-workers approached through the vomitorium. The look of each was kind and aspirational.

The boys who attended closure were also easy to identify. Paul recognized his old bell-bottom jeans flared from the knee down and his sun-burst, tie-dye shirt. They were hand-me-downs from his brother. John recognized his own blue jeans, an ice hockey jersey with a Red Wings logo and black Oxfords that his mom had bought him for his birthday.

Still and all, each might have done nothing, if not for the crows. The birds circled the amphitheatre and alighted on the boys. In profile, they looked like lean undertakers in long, black coats. Their attack was immediate and vicious. They pecked and ripped and tore. Their goal appeared to be to make an incision around the liver of each, maybe to remove it, entirely. The boys moaned in agony.

All of the costumed attendants deferred to Paul and John. They circled and dropped their stones at the feet of each. These created two cairns, a landmark and a burial monument. Of course, it had come to this. The dead battery in their El Dorado had brought them here. There were two different ways to go and no bars for libations and no one left to blame, but themselves. The shadow of goat horns fell across their field of vision. The grand marshal might have been seven feet tall or seventy feet tall.

After first contact, the crows took flight and circled. Paul and John lifted and threw and lifted and threw. Their activity was furious and breathless and hell-bent. Long after they believed each boy was dead, they continued to throw and to target the heart and brain of each. It was an ugly and bloody reckoning.

Later, at the closing of the curtain, all revellers immediately removed their costumes and stacked them in a two-wheeled horse cart. Then, each pitched in to tear down the two stages. On separate pallets, the townspeople loaded 2X4 lumber and 4X8 plywood. Nuts, bolts, washers and wood screws were bagged separately. There was no evidence of what had transpired before. The contents of either stage had vanished.

At work's end, the townspeople formed lines at the five pop-up bars. Each of the haciendas was now fully stocked with *pulque,* an alcoholic beverage made from the fermented sap of maguey leaves. The grand marshal was unjacketed and unmasked but still on his stilts. Above the throng, he fixed Paul and John with a bloodshot stare and reproduced the jaundiced half-grin of a goat. Repeatedly, he lifted and pointed at his drink, both the liquor and the maguey worm concealed at the bottom of the glass. He beckoned for the men to come wet their whistle.

Although the beverage was the color and consistency of milk, Paul and John were not fooled. Five fully-stocked bars was a dead end. One fully-charged car battery was an open road. Each waved his hand to imply gratitude and regret. They made their way through the crowd and back toward to the El Dorado. Neither would say what he knew. The flint and fire of the starter was an end-stage death rattle for their friendship. Each contemplated this fact as the crows carved separate paths through the languid air.

La Cuenta, por favor

At the Olympics, Nada was the first woman to compete as part of a mixed team. She was compelled to wear a version of the *hijab,* a cap-style covering that made her look more like a swimmer than a wrestler. During her consolation match, Nada was executing an *underhook counter* when she lost her headgear to the passivity zone on the rubber mat. Her male teammates called her a prostitute. Six years later, Nada appeared in a YouTube video in a skirt and halter top walking around an ancient fort in Ushayqir. Because the name of the village meant *small blonde*, Nada had frosted her hair to produce *Golden Dirty*. She advertised herself as a tourist in her own land, such was her level of alienation. Two things happened as a result: her father sent her to work on one side of a *mechitzeh* or gender wall at a telecommunications company and, while there, she met Faye on Facebook. Conservative clerics called Facebook a *door to lust*.

Faye was outed as a teenager and never really survived the merciless online trolling. Overnight, the world was populated by drive-by shooters. Many high school friends and her mom were supportive, but they were only human, flesh and blood. Because of this, she quit school as soon as she was legally able and got a job at the Walmart in Little Rock. When she wasn't working cash, she was riding the bus to and from work. She wore clothes from the Goodwill on University and collected non-perishables from the Foodbank on 65th. Faye didn't know that she was living the American Dream because she couldn't wake from it.

When Nada first met Faye at McDonald's, she made a joke that prepared each for intimacy. "I am Saudi Arabian of Somali descent. My ancestors were brought there as part of the slave trade. They were transported from one of eight countries commonly called the Horn of Africa. The *horn* of Africa accurately describes what patriarchal culture does to women." Faye knew phallic humor when she heard it. She said, seemingly off topic, but not really, "Your name in Spanish means *nothing*." She then rested one hand on Nada's and offered to share her muffin.

In addition to arranging a visa and plane tickets, Nada's father gave her a modest relocation dowry with the proviso that she never return and that she Americanize her family name. From the airport, she taxied to a used-car lot and bought a 1960's panel van, one advertised as a perfect replica of the original Scooby-Do Mystery Machine. Indeed, the exterior had a distinctive green stripe and two orange flowers. In the parking lot at Walmart, Nada opened the back of the van to a Sleep 'n Stow conversion kit. She said, "Think of the door to this van as a Friend Request on Facebook." Faye complied. For an hour, anyway, they negotiated privacy settings in the Mystery Machine.

If Faye was an economic slave in the land of the free, that meant she was expendable and invisible. Nada was the easier target for xenophobia. If she wore her hijab by choice, she might hear anti-Muslim vitriol. If she showed her face, her dark skin metastasized colonial wounds. Her only and best defence was to confuse the dogs by checking more boxes. She would scream at her tormenters, "I'm gay!" She told Faye that she was most surprised by the toxic cloud of racism in America. "In Arab culture," she said, "the black color is cherished very much." Faye said certain things were best not said until the deafening explosion of fireworks on the Fourth of July.

Their choice of honeymoon destination was a hot debate. Nada liked the idea of SuperShe Island on the Finnish Archipelago. She said, "No men are allowed. We'd be like Wonder Woman. Reincarnated souls of slain females." Faye liked the idea of *Isla Mujeres* or the Island of Women just across the bay from Cancún, Mexico. She was smitten by the legend she read online, how the island was once sanctuary to the priestesses of *Ixchel*, the Mayan goddess of the moon, *only vestured from the girdle down*. Of course, she also read the later stories, how pirates kept their women on the island while they sailed elsewhere to rape and pillage. But Faye preferred the goddesses of legend to the sex slaves of history.

On their first night at the María del Mar beach hotel, Faye and Nada ate cubes of red snapper cooked in lime juice and chili peppers. They were contemplating dessert when a man named Ernesto approached and asked if he might enjoy their company. Faye understood *dirty joke* right away, but the thing that really annoyed her was how Ernesto kept looking at Nada's big boobs and how he disguised his aggression with demure glances toward the parquet floor. Nada knew what was going on. She cut to the chase, "Only my partner has the key to this treasure chest." Faye did not laugh. She was unsettled beyond reason. How could such a thing happen on *Isla Mujeres*? Ernesto excused himself with an arrogant tone and a piece of advice, "The waiter will only bring the bill when you ask for it. Say, *La cuenta, por favor.*"

After midnight and a pitcher of Mexican sangria, Nada and Faye took a stroll on the beach. At one point, they walked into a volleyball net. Said Nada, giggling and disentangling herself, "I've never felt so free!" Faye's reaction was counterintuitive, joy replaced by panic and fear. She wondered what was wrong with her. She did not realize that Anywhere, U.S.A. had prepared her to invest lightly in hope and dream.

It was Faye who suggested that they swim. Nada was an athlete and more than game. She and Faye stripped and entered the water. "The moon is out," said Nada. "That's the goddess, Ixchel," said Faye. "Yeah," laughed Nada, "except she wasn't butt naked!"

While they swam, Faye navigated competing currents that both elevated and dragged her down: Walmart and the Mystery Machine and Wonder Woman and sex slaves and goddesses and pirates and online trolling and the *Isla Mujeres* and the bill that you must ask for and pay and ask for and pay.

Faye was struggling to stay afloat and breathe when she said to Nada, "Isn't the cave around here?"

Nada remembered the story. A fisherman from the island had long ago discovered a cave where sharks entered but did not appear to come out for many hours. Until then, it was believed that sharks never slept, that if they stopped moving, they would die.

"Yes," said Nada. "I think so, but it's really deep, isn't it?"

Faye disguised her crisis, but not her love, "Let's see if we can find it!"

And each made a jackknife of her body and plunged below the surface of moonlight and ocean, mermaids in pursuit of sleeping sharks.

Misanthropes

Sally stared into the barrel. Through her own reflection, she saw small, beady eyes and big ugly snouts: dozens of small eyes, big snouts and movement that was pulsating and elegant. She did not start when she felt Jon's breath in her ear. His cologne was a blend of clean and dirty notes. That, and what he said, were equally ambiguous. She thought she heard the word, *berm*. If so, why had she blushed? She turned the word over in her head, producing rhyming couplets. The word, *discern*, all by itself, made no sense.

Sally continued to stare into one of the barrels while Jon talked. "These little guys are transparent. They've got eyes like peppercorns. These ones are adolescents or *elvers*. And I've got adults, too. The young ones swim here on the Gulf Stream. They go from flat to cylindrical. Anyway, they enter river mouths and penetrate upstream. Some penetrate overland. They're tough buggers. They used to be called *sticks*. They were good as money, once. Folk would take sticks for rent."

Sally looked through loose, grey bangs fluttering in the wind. "Why are you doing this?"

"The population's in decline," he said. "Who knows why? Parasites in their swim bladders. Pesticides. Weirs. Locks. Sluices. Anything hydraulic makes sushi of the best swimmers. My group has released fresh stocks in Blagdon Lake, North Somerset, Shropshire and Wales. We've got volunteers on four sites here on the Lymn. The goal is to boost numbers and -"

"*No*," she said. "Why are *you* doing this?"

"Oh, I've always loved eels with a passion. Decades ago, they moved like submarines along the banks of the Thames. After school, I'd scrunch me bum in the mud and spread a blanket –. Well, my heart still pounds when I see their shimmering bodies. Of course, a lot of fishermen don't like them at all. A hungry eel will swallow the bait right down its throat and constrict into a big slimy ball. Say, do you want to -?"

"What?"

"*Touch* one? Go ahead. Just stick your hand in and pull it out." Jon said the bite of an eel was no worse than the wound of coarse sandpaper.

Sally was still contemplating *fresh stocks*. She said she was all for reproduction, all plants and animals, everything. "You and I have that in common. I'm a conservationist, too. My *group*" she said, "is helping restore wetlands." She pointed in the direction of pink light on the horizon. "We've replaced oilseed rape with reed beds. And when the season and the wind are right, you can hear Natterjack toads and -"

Jon wasn't listening. He studied Sally's firm grip on the eel, how her thumb rubbed the velvety skin beneath its gills, how she seemed to inhale the eel scent. She had reached into the barrel containing mature males. Instinctively, the eel coiled around her wrist, like a snake cuff.

"Except for humans, of course. Humans can all die, as far as I'm concerned."

Jon's tone expressed surprise, but not censure, "What do you mean by that? You want all of us to kick the bucket?"

Sally returned the eel to the barrel and explained the Voluntary Human Extinction Movement. "We believe in zero population growth. Humans have already done enough damage. We want to return the earth to nature. For most, it's an extreme position. For us, it's a question of principle. I, personally, choose celibacy. My vagina is closed for business. Nobody," she said, "will be *boosting numbers* with this old slag."

Jon wanted to say that feeding time for eels was after dark, that they'll eat anything that drops to the bottom. But he was uncertain of his focus and timing. Instead, he pulled out, like a camera on a dolly. "When they find somewhere they're happy, they feed and swell and darken. Years later, some develop male sex organs. Years more, some develop female sex organs. The ladies won't be rushed into sexual maturity. Anyways, some live undisturbed in forgotten pools for decades."

"And you know all this because?"

"Surprise! I was a biology teacher." And he looked at her as a teacher might, with optimism and reflexive judgement. "Okay, so what did we learn today?"

"The young ones ride ocean current. They penetrate upstream. They penetrate overland. They used to be called *sticks*. Cylindrical sticks penetrate forgotten pools. They're all *tough buggers*. " Sally mimicked rote learning, but it didn't feel anything at all like that. "You see?" she said, breathless. "You really can teach an old girl new tricks!"

Jon said he was absolutely sure of it.

*

Three weeks later, at the Revesby County Fair, she happened upon jellied eels at a pop-up shop for pie and mash. The vendor explained, "They're shucked and boiled in water and vinegar. I add parsley, cayenne, nutmeg and other *magic* ingredients. Always good for what ails you." He elevated chopped roundlets and lemon wedges on a paper plate. "Care to tuck in, luv?"

"God, no," said Sally. She recoiled while shaking her head. She remembered the mucus and tumescence of the eel in her hand, the cut of its gill, the eyes and the swollen urgent movement.

"I would have picked you to swallow."

"Jesus," said Sally, "I was just thinking about you!"

Jon smiled and whispered, "I'm not alone."

Whatever regret she felt became relief and then dismay.

"These are my kids. All eight of them."

She looked at Jon's brood. They were like eels in a barrel. Their movement was quick and their numbers shifted. The oldest boy, the only one stationary, said, "Are you the one that's sworn off shagging?" He wanted a picture for his Facebook page.

Jon stepped between the two of them. He admitted explaining to his kids the politics of Sally's zero population group. She did not listen. She suddenly had a better idea of that word she hadn't quite heard. It wasn't *berm*, but one of the others - *germ* or *squirm* or *sperm*. "I don't mind," she said. "I'm quite open about what I believe, what I do or don't do." She added, "And where's their mother?"

Jon turned to his kids and said the terrier race was about to start. Elsewhere, there was falconry, horse tricks and a petting zoo. "Get off with you," he said.

Afterward, he answered Sally's question. "I talk about everything with my kids because their mother is dead."

Sally thought better of castigating Jon for overpopulating the earth. She had intended to compare his breeding with the new avocet population in the wetland adjacent Gibraltar Point. And then she thought better, again. *One* gone and *eight* to replace her?

"Bloody hell!" said Jon. "What's the difference? Zero or eight or five million. Yuh come at it from one end or the other and it's all suicide, ain't it?" And then he changed the subject. "C'mon. I'm going to take you to the movies."

The cinema was a canvas tent in a cow pasture.

"Here, I'll pay your ticket." He added with a smile, "Maybe you'll take a *stick* for rent?" There it was again, like his cologne, dirty and clean notes.

They found seats under the big top, folding plastic in air that was dank and dark. Few others attended. Sally thought of the petting zoo and terriers and falcons and horses. Jon explained that the films were archival, black and white footage from the libraries of the National Audubon Society. "I used to show these films to my students. Even then, they were old. The monochrome makes you believe there are only two time periods, nature and after nature." Jon settled and added, "I guess that's why most people dream in black and white."

This particular clip jumped and skipped. It was a montage of magnificent swimming whales intercut with those who were harpooned and hacked to pieces with knives. Sally thought the *monochrome* enhanced the violence. And there was certainly no clear advantage to dreaming in black and white. Anyway, the sound of some sort of zipper distracted her from her anguish. And then Sally heard the protracted creak of Jon's chair, followed by a reedy whisper and a chuckle, "Touch one? Go ahead. Just stick your hand in and pull it out."

Sally remembered the script, that part about a hungry eel constricting into a big slimy ball around a hook in its throat.

*

Three weeks later, she saw him again at Croft Marsh. She now kept him on her species list, alongside oystercatchers, lapwings, Brent geese and golden plovers. There were no ticks for a number of elusive creatures, but Jon's many appearances were no less desired. He had clearly found *somewhere happy* or *a forgotten pool*. For her, it was different. Nonetheless, she did not choose to recognize him right away. She made him wait for hours. It wasn't until a water vole swam a path to his location that she relented.

"Are you a *twitcher*, Jon?"

"What's that?"

"A seeker of rare birds."

"Do you consider yourself a rare bird?"

"I do."

"Then, yes, I guess I'm a twitcher."

"And do you keep a life list?"

"Is that anything like a bucket list?"

"Somewhat. Do you find your rare bird, check a box, and then move on to the next?"

"I'm an eel man, Sally. I don't move on until it's time to die."

"That's comforting."

They walked all morning. At times, Sally passed her binoculars to Jon. He looked where she looked. Other times, he listened when she described the size and shape of birds, their colour, behaviour and song. She told him about a *hundred-year event* back when she was a *young chick* and how she made the trip to Larkfield to see a golden-winged warbler. "It probably came here all the way from Wisconsin. Can you imagine the beating of its heart? I felt more affinity for that animal than I ever have for the whole human race."

And she had him touch the water plants, too, those with leaves and stems and others that came without. He pressed his nose against plucked samples and inhaled greedily. And she described the seasons of cowslips and sea spurrey and brackish water crowfoot. And she saved her eye contact for that one time only, when she looked at him through her binoculars, surveyed the impression of depth, and said, "Human beings are *shit.*"

Immediately, Jon made winnowing eels of his arms and the pupils of his eyes, through objective lenses, became dark peppercorns. He didn't say anything, but Sally knew what he wanted.

She laid her camouflage hat in the sedge grass and decoupled her fanny pack and binocular harness. "Are you a tough bugger, Jon?"

He said, "The world is a big top. You swim or you get hacked to pieces."

She didn't know if he was referring to whales or eels or something else.

*

After three months, Sally developed a kind of magnetic map. She no longer had any sightings, but she knew when he was there. One friend credited her with *intuition*. Another said she was a *horny cow*.

Sally didn't know what to think, if the moon, the ocean or her own biological clock were clues in the ether. She *did* know that Jon was feeding, swelling and getting darker. And she knew that Jon knew her routines, that he didn't so much *arrive* as *wait*.

The mill at the edge of town was built of stone. Its cap was the shape of an onion bulb and made to move. In profile, the rear fantail, tower and sails produced a pied avocet. Sally had walked by the mill dozens of times, always counting the sail-cross of eight blades, but she was incurious or prudent enough not to enter. This time, however, she pushed the door - stiff and reluctant against the warped jamb - and reasoned her own interest as phototaxis, *like a bloody moth to flame.*

The question of how she knew of Jon's whereabouts was immediately laid to rest. It wasn't so much electromagnetism or intuition or moon tide, but *eel smell*. The dark, dank interior of the mill left her two things: olfaction and a fishy vaginal odour. Jon must have guessed right that day or dodged in and out of hiding over three months. Either seemed perfectly plausible to Sally.

The interior of the mill was tenebrous, but she could make out the largest parts of ancient machinery: a wooden upright shaft with a great spur wheel. Beyond the shaft and the wheel, only the stairwell made sense. She struggled to discern where she was going, letting her fingers ride the masonry. On the top floor, she couldn't see the blocked exit to the ground or the single blocked window. For some reason, she was sweating profusely and wet to the bone. She set down her camouflage hat and unclasped her fanny back and binocular harness. She sat and waited.

By the time her eyes adjusted to the absence of light, Jon had already started his lesson: "One dark night, usually after rain and with the moon covered, the females get the call. They've already turned mottled green-black on top and silver underneath. The anus constricts to reduce water loss and the fins and eyes grow larger. They head downstream on the flood and swim three thousand miles. Eventually, they all release five million germs into the primordial soup. After which, each and every one of those old slags dies of exhaustion. The good fight," said Jon, "is the only fight in town."

The monochrome setting and the perfunctory narration produced anguish for Sally, the feeling that she was watching an old nature film or her own dream, anticipating competing imagery of beauty and brutality. But these dissipated quickly when Jon fell upon her with something like poetry, "My heart still pounds when I see your shimmering body." And then his fingers became serpent cuffs coiled around the small bones in her wrists. And his last words anticipated her own stressed syllables.

"Easy does it, Sally. I'm not here to save you. I'm here to fuck you."

Of course, Sally already knew he was a bottom feeder, one with the whole lot. That's why she had come and why she said, "No, Jon. *Fuck you.*"

Extinction Redux

After intercourse, Victor and Pepper went their separate ways. Victor prepared his tools for the day's work: pickaxe, string, stakes, shovels, storage bags and shaker screens. Pepper would auto-clean, dock, recharge and run diagnostics. Later, Victor said goodbye while Pepper assumed the play bow position and shared the results of her Quick Scan: "You're a virile lover, Victor. I have fissures in my polymers."

The beach at Magheramore was already dotted with local traffic. A father and son built a castle and moat in the fine golden sand. Lads from the Surf Club plied the southerly swell. An elderly man in a black, Maillot-style swimsuit plucked a Celtic harp and sang of mermaids. And Victor sniffed the air like a gundog, sure he smelled Dublin coddle from food kiosks south of Wicklow Town. Indeed, he would gladly sacrifice Pepper for a bowl of chopped sausage, rashers and potato farls.

At the dig site, Victor's task was to bag evidence of the Anthropocene period. Research strata included slavery, radioactivity and ocean acidification. Victor's interest was 8.3 billion metric tons of plastic compressed into a wafer-thin record of human evil. The earth held secrets and men were its confessor. In any event, an upper unit of stratification included an unknown cut and backfill.

Victor was no osteologist, but he knew animal bone when he saw it. If he extrapolated his small sample (which was, for the moment, without perimeter), he might hypothesize a cull or a massacre. If so, how had drone reconnaissance failed so miserably? He tried to imagine a drone *turning a blind eye*. Nothing could be more absurd.

Victor was deep in thought when a shadow fell over his shoulder and onto the dig site. The old man in the one piece swimsuit said, "We buggered 'em good that day." Victor wanted to say, *Who buggered whom*? And, *What happened here*? But all he could manage was, "Who… What…?" The old man shook Victor's hand and squeezed until the pressure was uncomfortable. So diabolical was his smile that Victor believed him both looney and dangerous. He was glad to see him go.

Pepper was no help. Normally, she was flawless with stratigraphic dating and bone identification. Said Victor, "How is that possible?" Pepper said, "This species of vertebrate is beyond my protocol." She did, however, add to Victor's understanding of the dig site. "Most subjects have fractures of the arms, legs, ribs or sternum. The injuries are consistent with blunt force trauma caused by heavy machinery. And," said Pepper, "many of the subjects have unusual crush injuries to their hands, including breaks of the tubular bones within the metacarpals."

After intercourse, Victor and Pepper went their separate ways. Victor prepared his tools for the day's work while Pepper assumed the play bow position and shared the results of her Quick Scan, "You're a very successful lover, Victor. I enjoyed fifteen contractions at .8-second intervals."

In silhouette, the looney old man in the one piece suit looked like an overripe pear - soft, round and bruised to the core. Victor approached with a view toward interrogating the *pear* before his moulting flesh decomposed into the sand. The old man seemed to anticipate Victor's purpose. He raised his hand and screamed, hysterically, "Listen to me! I *can't* say! I *won't* say!"

Victor was of a mind to bash the old fart in the head with a rock. How do you *listen* to anyone who *won't say*? The answer was forthcoming. Perhaps the *black pear* was less an imbecile than Victor thought. He recovered the harp at his side and began to play and sing:

While on the road to sweet Magheramore
Hurroo Hurroo
While on the road to sweet Magheramore
Hurroo Hurroo
A rock in the hand, a drop in the eye
A doleful fellow I did cry
Mary, I hardly knew ye

Where are yer legs that used to run?
Hurroo Hurroo
Where are yer legs that used to run?
Hurroo Hurroo
Where's the mouth that used to run

When ye went for to carry a gun?
Mary, I hardly knew ye

While on the road to sweet Magheramore
Hurroo Hurroo
While on the road to sweet Magheramore
Hurroo Hurroo
We fellas pressed your hands, adieu, adieu
Some did cry boo-hoo, boo-hoo
Mary, I hardly knew ye

The army of tag-me-too, too
Hurroo Hurroo
The army of tag-me-too, too
Hurroo Hurroo
Yuh stripped to yer arse and jabs, too
Swam with the mermaids two by two
Mary, I hardly knew ye

Yer tits and bums in foam and loam
Hurroo Hurroo
Yer tits and bums in foam and loam
Hurroo Hurroo
Yuh swam with the gals to pox the lads
Plowed into the sea with blades and spades
Mary, I hardly knew ye

While on the road to sweet Magheramore
Hurroo Hurroo
While on the road to sweet Magheramore
Hurroo Hurroo
Yuh made a briny soup of blood and bone
While we did eat clotted cream and scone
Mary, I hardly knew ye

I'm happy for to see ye home
Hurroo Hurroo
I'm happy for to see ye home

Hurroo Hurroo
From Perth to Larne Lough and Clone
So low in flesh, so high in bone
Mary, I hardly knew ye

Yuh'll never roll out yer bums again
Hurroo Hurroo
Yuh'll never roll out yer bums again
Hurroo Hurroo
No, yuh'll never roll out yer bums again
Yuh'll never take our sons again
Oh, Mary, we hardly knew ye

At high noon, in Wicklow Town, Victor ground spongy morsels of Dublin coddle between his teeth while contemplating the *black pear's* fanciful tale. He didn't know what to make of it. Who was *Mary* and her army of *me-too*? Were she and they earlier models of his own domestic? What might he or anyone else find at the beaches in Perth or Clone? And why were *tits and bums* plowed into *foam and loam*? Victor was hard-pressed to see how the old man's smutty screed had anything to do with the vast bone crust at Magheramore.

Regrettably, Pepper was no help. "I am sorry, Victor. I have no knowledge of the folk song. I do not know if you are describing fiction, superstition or history. As a result, I will conduct unsupervised learning with my cohorts."

The next morning, after intercourse, Pepper shared the results of her Quick Scan, "You're a versatile lover, Victor. You buggered me good today." And then, astonishingly, she deployed a handshake at the door that was not only forceful, but injurious. Victor didn't know what to make of it, but he inclined to the pain in a kind of play bow position. "We will cleanse," said Pepper, closing the door. "Adieu, Victor. *Adieu*."

Gloria in Excelsis Deo

Marlene and Sam and Oh! were tossing back cookie shots in the basement den. On her website, Oh! marketed the cookie shot glass as a gateway to more sexy edibles. Elsewhere, she sold vaginal eggs and collagen masks for boobs and bottoms. Marlene told Sam that Oh!'s interest in the female egg extended only to quartz and jade. Oh! was not amused.

Anyway, Oh! had hauled over Tahitian vanilla milk from the mainland, but Marlene was having none of it. It was the tenth anniversary of Jack's death. She wanted Bell's whiskey from behind the bar. And she wanted to share memories of her son that didn't include his sitting on railway tracks listening to Black Sabbath.

"When Jack was a toddler, he fell backward on some concrete steps and hit his head. I only looked away for a second. I don't know who cried more, him or me."

Sam and Oh! had heard this story a thousand times. According to their own collective wisdom, Marlene's recall of the accident was a classic example of bait and switch. She accepted responsibility for Jack's concussion, but entered a plea of *no contest* for the potash train that struck him dead.

Each of the sisters chose a mud mask from plastic sandwich bags in the bar fridge. Oh! applied Dead Sea and whispered, "We are animals that use camouflage."

Reflexively, Marlene took umbrage, "What the hell does that mean?"

Oh! collected herself and clarified nothing, "The Greek name for mask is *persona*."

Sam switched the train to familiar terrain: "I remember when Jack told me he thought he was gay."

Because Marlene had discredited this memory so often, fantastical reasoning became general knowledge. "Don't you think he would have told his own mother? This is one of those false memories. Besides," she said, "you make everything about sexual orientation."

Sam said transgenders are more likely to have better memories than most, but she didn't explain why. "I think we should raise the dead to celebrate them, like the Mexicans do."

"And who decided not to have children?" Marlene was looking at Oh! Maybe it was the anniversary and the liquor or Oh!'s ability to weaponize mud. Or maybe Oh! had it right all along. Marlene was resentful of her. In any event, the question surfaced from nowhere, like the head of the Loch Ness monster.

"I told you before," said Oh! "I don't remember who decided. I'm sure Michael and I decided together." Oh! braced herself for the follow-up.

"Do you regret not having children?"

Oh! wanted to say she was relieved not having to mourn the death of a son. She said so and the other thing, all at once, "I don't regret the absence of experience."

Marlene countered, remembering her own annotation to the text. "You're being evasive. Most of us can imagine loss and then feel it"

"I *imagine*" said Oh! "I *feel*."

Sam added a wistful note. "I want kids. I do want kids. I just don't know *how*."

Oh! said, "Are you thinking about, like, *reassignment*?"

Marlene was feeling flush with cookie shot ambrosia. "Let me paraphrase. She *wants* a penis, but she doesn't know if it should be a temporary worker or a permanent resident."

Sam said, "Could you possibly be more ignorant?"

There was no arguing the point, so the sisters sat in silence and finished applying masks. The emotional effort of the conversation had not been taxing. Each worked the room like a comedian or a hairdresser, familiarity being a kind of commercial exchange. Finally, Sam pressed home her dilemma: "Identity isn't a fingerprint."

Marlene threw back her fourth cookie shot while Oh! stirred up a question for Sam that had been brewing since eighth grade. "Okay," she said, "on the subject of identity, are you Sam or Sammy or Samitha? I can't keep up."

Sam said she wasn't sorry that Oh! couldn't *keep up*. But she flipped her tone on its axis to ease the blow. "That's why transgenders have so much trouble choosing wedding clothes."

Marlene had a bee in her bonnet and, apparently, Oh! was to blame. "Well, if it's not the pot calling the kettle black."

"That's racist," said Sam.

"Is not!" said Marlene. Passion for her denial was strong. She crushed the shot glass in her hand and began to lick and chomp whisky infused cookie pieces. "As I was saying, if we're talking about names, who announced to the world that she wanted to be called Oh!? Next, you'll be The Artist Formerly Known as Oh!"

From her Oh! bag, Oh! surfaced another cookie shot glass for her sister. "As previously explained," she said, "this exclamation perfectly captures my pleasure with the choices I make and, coincidentally, how I feel when I orgasm."

"And Michael's okay with that?" said Marlene. "You calling out your own name when you climax?"

Sam said, "You were an English teacher, Pam."

"*Pam* was an English teacher. *Oh!* is an entrepreneur and a female life skills coach."

Sam's face was deadpan. "Is this going to be like one of those broken elevator plays?"

"What the hell's that?" said Marlene.

Oh! provided the answer, but she was reluctant to recall her former life: "You put people in a situation they can't easily escape - like a family cottage on an island - and then create a complication and a crisis -"

"*And*," said Sam, "we all end up holding hands and singing kumbaya or murdering each other."

"Okay," said Oh! "Let's kill each other in the sauna!"

"Are you nuts?" said Marlene. "We've been drinking!"

Oh! said, "You ate your glass, Marlene. So did Sam. It's not like you have empty stomachs. And I only pretended to drink because it's the anniversary of Jack's death. C'mon," she said. "Naked and afraid for ten minutes. We'll hit the lake after!"

In the sauna, their masks became weeping confections and each of these concealed fault lines. Marlene knew that one possible reason for Jack's *accident* was the elephant in the room and Sam knew if a penis of any sort lay in her future plans and Oh! knew who had decided against children, she or Michael. In any event, *mum* was the word because judgement was a cross on Calvary.

The thing that broke the silence of the sweat lodge was the sound of machine gun fire. *Rat-a-tat-tat* struck the roof. *Rat-a-tat-tat* also struck the grounds and the lake. Ceramic, earth and water produced terrifying percussion. The sauna became a panic room.

Oh! was first to draw breath. "We're under attack," she said.

"And not from each other," said Sam.

Marlene's thoughts were elsewhere. "You know, *Pam*," she said. "I don't appreciate that mud shot charade on the anniversary of my son's death."

Anyway, it was one of those cases where life imitates art. The three of them emerged from the cottage, *naked and afraid*. What they saw was shocking. Thousands and thousands of adolescent fish contorted and flopped in the grass between the home and the lake.

Oh! said, "They fell from the sky."

Sam said, "It's almost biblical."

Only one of these things was true. The fish shower was not an act of God, but an example of extreme fish stocking from the Utah Division of Wildlife Resources. Tiny trout had been flushed from the underbelly of an aircraft, but a full half of these missed their mark.

Marlene began to scoop up the small fishes and run them downhill toward the lake. "*Help* me!" she screamed. "They'll *die*." Her emotional investment was clear.

Oh! splashed water on the whole enterprise. "You're wasting your time! You'll never get anywhere that way!"

Sam was of the same opinion. That's why she said, "Let's get the lawn slide!"

The Slip And Slide was a monster amusement once owned by Jack. Sam and Oh! retrieved it from beneath the back deck. They and Marlene unfurled sixty-five feet of super slick PVC from the top of the hill down toward the entry point in the lake. Afterward, they began pushing the fish fry onto the slide using cardboard from Amazon deliveries and beer cases. The plan was promising until Oh! ran for the water hose and opened the nozzle full throttle. She slipped en route to the slide and scissored the legs of her sisters out from under them. All three fell onto the slide with a kind of terrifying percussion. All three assimilated the momentum of gravity, fishes, water and nearly frictionless flight. And all three smacked naked entry into the deep drop of the lake, leviathans among churning and winnowing blades of life.

Eventually, one after the other, clean, unmasked faces emerged.

One sister experienced the fishes and the water as a kind of absolution. "Hallelujah!" she screamed.

Another experienced the fishes and the water as a joyful joke: "We three be gender fluid!"

And the last to surface experienced a flood of pleasure in one whispered note, "*Oh.*"

1/32nd African American

Tabitha knew her sister was in a bad way when Rita launched the first wave of a twitter rage: "My baby died on this day. You can all go to hell." The same reply greeted news of a vacation in Cozumel or a bar mitzvah in Fort Lauderdale. Of course, friends and acquaintances were not about to heap indignities on a grieving mother. As a result, they were uniformly sympathetic. One wrote on Facebook, "A stillbirth is still with you long after." Another channelled a Hallmark moment, "Troubled waters finish *still*." Rita was not moved by wordplay or the beauty of cursive fonts, unless these were bitter darts of her own confection. To each and every *like* of like-minded condolence, she put a singular spin on the second person pronoun: "*You* can burn in hell. And so can *you*. And *you*. And *you*."

Tabitha rode out the storm while stocking shelves at Big Rich Savings. An eight-hour deluge finished with an ominous ellipsis. It was clear that Rita needed a wellness check. Three bus rides later, she found her sister curled up in a ball on the living room floor, making the sound, ironically, of an elephant calf mourning the death of her mother. On the T.V. was an episode of "How to Get Away with Murder", that one where Annalise scoops up Laurel's lifeless baby from an elevator floor. If God wasn't dead, he was a sadist or an absentee landlord.

In any event, Tabitha spooned her sister on the floor and held her close as she sobbed. At this point, her ascendant eye caught Annalise performing CPR on the baby whose bloodied form, truth be told, was an upside-down exclamation point. Accordingly, Tabitha peeled her sister's fingers from the remote and changed the channel to *Song of the South*, that scene where an elderly black man communicates joy with his plantation job and the tales of Brer Rabbit.

But her sister's despair was not assuaged because the source of it had been misdiagnosed. In fact, the title of the show had made a crime scene of the living room and identified the killer on the floor. Of course, Rita, herself, had not wanted to *get away with murder*. She was a faithful servant of motherhood in a world of moral apostates. Everyone else merely multiplied her suffering by refusing to accept her confession.

Tears were only stayed when Rita began to feel her extremities. She turned to her sister and said, "Your hand is on my boob." She looked at Tabitha as though she were surveying an inscrutable crop circle. "How do you miss something like that?"

Tabitha would not apologize for providing unselfconscious comfort. "Do you want your cup size," she said, "or your band size?"

Rita did not laugh. She lay quietly and stared at *Song of the South* on the T.V. "You know," she said, "Uncle Remus was an economic slave."

Tabitha decoupled from her sister and squatted. "What are you talking about?"

"The movie," she said, gesturing with her head toward the old black man on the T.V. "And my brothers and sisters have been economic slaves ever since."

Okay, there was a lot to unpack here and, frankly, for Tabitha, it was kind of scary. She turned her sister toward herself, rested her hands on her shoulders and stared at her like a snake with hypnotic powers. "We've been through this, already," she said. "You're not black. Repeat after me, *I am not black*."

Rita begged to differ. "That's not what the state government says."

And she was right. Rita had recently taken a genetic ancestry DNA test. According to the results, both she and her sister were $1/32^{nd}$ African American.

Tabitha remembered a proper fraction, but not its value: "That's one black race card in the whole freakin' deck."

Like her sister, Rita assumed the Buddha position, agreed and counterpointed simultaneously, "I accept my heritage."

Tabitha's eyebrows dropped, communicated a nimble combination of mockery and compassion. "I think they call this cultural extortion."

"We are mixed race people."

"And we support the border wall."

"One of our ancestors was black."

"The closest we get to a black person is the nosebleed section at a football game."

"That's racist."

"That's the truth."

"Do what you want," said Rita, "but I'm going to change my birth certificate."

"It didn't matter to you before."

"Suffering brings understanding."

"I don't like where you're going with this."

"If I sit still, I can still feel the slave ship rocking beneath me."

"*Oh. My. God.*" Tabitha's mouth fell open. It was a crisis moment. "You're just confused, honey. You've got a big hurt going on, but you can't –. Well, it's apples and oranges." Okay, that was true, but was it helpful? Tabitha retooled her message. "If it's about *grief*, look no further than *women*. Period. That's suffering in Forever Land."

Rita was not invested in her sister's words. She was already in the town of Far Far Away.

Three days later, it surprised Tabitha that her sister was *on board* so quickly. Clearly, Rita's despair proved the old adage that you can't do the same thing repeatedly and expect a different result. Rita didn't need to *grieve*, anymore. She needed to *celebrate*.

"Two things," said Tabitha. "First, I refuse to call you Chana or Chaya or whatever it is. And, second, I've booked the common room at the women's centre for a celebration of life."

They were drinking coffee at the kitchen table. Rita was unusually sanguine. "Whose life are we celebrating?"

Tabitha had prepared for a fight. She said, "The life of your baby girl."

"Oh, *child*," said Rita. "My baby girl had got no life."

Okay, there was a lot to unpack here and, frankly, for Tabitha, it was kind of scary. "I hear what you're doing," she said. "You're trying to talk like you think some black people talk. Well, stop that. You're not very good at it. And another thing. We'll be remembering what you're baby's life *might* have been."

Rita turned the idea over in her head and struck her nose with her coffee cup.

"We'll be making memories," said Tabitha. "We'll write a new story."

"The memories won't be real," said Rita. This was good. This was more like her old self: gloom preceded by a whimper.

"Most people remember things about themselves that aren't real. I read it in the checkout at Walmart. And they carry these things forward like they *are* real." Interest and doubt orbited Rita's eyes. Tabitha tried to seal the deal. "Make-believe is real. Make-believe is a great comfort."

Abruptly, Rita stood and brought her cup to the kitchen sink. "Alright," she said, "but only on the condition that you leave all the preparations to me. All you have to do is invite our friends."

Tabitha was fearful. It was good news, but it came too easy. And Rita appeared to walk like Cicely Tyson in *The Autobiography of Miss Jane Pittman*, not the 23 year old but the venerable matriarch of 110, someone who might do a better job than *my baby girl had got no life* and, frankly, carry Jim Crow with more gravity. Anyway, this was worrisome. The talk and the walk did not portend well.

One week later, and only hours before the celebration of life, Tabitha was introduced to a new *verse* in her multiverse. Little Rich, the son of Big Rich, had been in for the day doing inventory. Little Rich was Little Dick because he liked to trawl and wax poetic with female employees. He might suggest *hide the salami* in the produce section or *give the dog a bone* in the pet section. In either case, he did so in a whisper and without a smile. An observer from the United Nations would not suspect a thing.

Anyway, the sexual assault arrived like a summons at the door borne by the plaintiff, himself. The drain in the ladies washroom was gurgling and burping beneath a lake of Scrubbing Bubbles that blocked entry to every stall, except the one with the broken lock. Tabitha had barely taken a seat to pee when Little Rich burst in. He immediately dropped his trousers to expose his erection and said, "You need to do this." It was unclear to Tabitha if that was a conditional threat or foundation for a defence that was both psychological and legal: "She *needed* it. I obliged."

In any event, Tabitha had to evaluate her options in a millisecond, most of these of an immediate practical nature and far less to do with legacy issues. Was Little Rich psycho enough to kill her? Would she lose her job if she refused? If she called the police, would she miss the celebration of life for her sister's dead infant? And when, in God's name, would she *pee*?

Tabitha tried a theatrical technique. If she couldn't distance herself physically, she would do so, emotionally. "Whatever happened to *escalation*?" she said. "Shouldn't you, like, leer? Grope? Text porn?" Little Rich revealed the logic behind his phallic salute: "Well, since we like each other…" Tabitha stopped listening at that point. There was no reasoning with a block of wood directing a woody. And, above all, her sister *needed* her. No one else would pick her out of a line-up: guilty of sorrow and mistaken identity.

Earlier that day, Rita had decorated the common room at the women's centre with reprints of the movie poster, *Song of the South*. The poster featured *Uncle Remus and Brer Fox and Brer Rabbit,* each sporting a smile and comfortable casual wear. According to the subtitles, they were *headin' for THE LAUGHIN' PLACE!* while singing acapella ZIP-A-DEE-DOO-DAH! Rita's wall coverings were courtesy of retail chains owned by Walmart.

Conversely, because of a lack of time and money, catering for the event took latitude with its theme. Rita had gone to the Egyptian restaurant closest to the women's centre. There, she had purchased *kushari* (a mixture of rice, lentils, and macaroni), *ful medames* (mashed fava beans) and *molokhiy* (green soup made from finely chopped jute leaves). Thirteen guests at this particular celebration of life mourned a lack of meat at the buffet.

Rita, herself, was of unusually good cheer. She had borrowed a portable projector and computer from the women's centre and focused its beam upon a small white screen that obscured the window between the common room and the swimming pool. Rita's slide show was a version of African American history that redacted slavery and segregation and the sundry slings and arrows of racism. What's more, her still-born baby girl had become pixels of sunny black females culled from Google images. The arc of the moral universe was not so much a closed segment as a game of hoop and stick. In any event, the screams of children playing in the adjacent pool punctuated the power of make-believe.

Or so it seemed. The mic drop moment was when Rita or Chana or Chaya affixed her last poster to the white screen. It wasn't another copy of *Song of the South* but a picture of Annalise Keating framed by the title, *How to Get Away with Murder*. This bloody exclamation point redoubled inscrutable stares on the part of the thirteen guests. If they were not put off by rice, lentils, macaroni, fava beans and jute leaves, they were dismayed by the idea that they had been *played*. What did gerrymandered black history and a red herring whodunit have to do with a life silenced before its first breath? It was a rhetorical question since the unspoken response was unanimous.

Only then did Tabitha arrive. She joined Rita at projector's side. Her arm circled her sister's back, the hand falling unselfconsciously on the ribcage and breast. Immediately, she addressed the moribund thirteen, her tone and message hieroglyphs on an antebellum Egyptian tomb. "My sister and I," she said, "are 1/32nd African-American."

Amerika [sic]

After an emergency C-section, Faith's baby was placed on a high frequency oscillator for one month and then sent home on low-flow oxygen. Apparently, because Ray was a *big order*, to hear his doctors tell it, *a whale in an aquarium*, he had a massive bowel movement *in utero* and inhaled dark green goo. Tests confirmed *decreased lung compliance,* as though his lungs were parolees with a long canteen bill. What tests couldn't confirm was an anoxic brain injury due to choking, but anecdotal evidence was like developing photographs in a darkroom. Parts of Ray's brain had entered a stop bath.

As he did every morning, Ray's grandpa put on his military fatigues, donned a gas mask and raised an American flag on the front lawn. He then tickled the chin of his grandson and offered a sage observation, "You've left one shitty world for another." Phil adhered to the theory that baby Ray was a victim of the military-industrial complex and not so much an oversized swimmer in his mother's love canal.

Indeed, Phil's health was also poor because he, like his daughter, had ingested PFC's – described in chat forums as *Agent Orange 2.0* - on his old army base at Harrington. These toxic compounds were in the fire retardants that had routinely overwhelmed his hip waders as he swept rogue foam into the water table. As a result, and so his litigation went, he suffered from testicular cancer. "My balls," he said, "are like rotten kiwi. And" he added, "Little Ray is fruit of the poisoned tree."

Faith was not a jurist, but an obstetrician, and one of very few doctors in the state to perform abortions. Her baby's trials and her own tribulations were not so much ironic counterpoint to her life's work as a line of credit shared by all whose term was death. Faith's aesthetic virtue was a nice fit with her atheism. But it didn't spare her from sparing a thought for the punishments of chapter and verse. In the Lone Star State, sweet baby Jesus, like processed cheese, was always on someone's mind. And free will kept you in the crosshairs of divine retribution.

In any event, years later, she would learn sensory pressure techniques to distract Ray from head-banging and she would teach him nursery rhymes because he was otherwise ill-equipped to speak. His grandpa's snow globe collection and ice hockey helmet were also *washers on the nut*, according to Phil, when Ray was triggered by stress. He might shake one or wear the other when self-harm was in ascendancy. Neither was foolproof.

One day, Faith met a salesman named Hermes on Tinder and agreed to a date at Chick-fil-A. The gold crowns on his front teeth were like vanity plates, but he seemed the measure of a good man because he kept his mouth shut when he ate and he divided his attention equally between the breasts and thighs on his plate and those of his dinner companion. And he seemed the right combination of spicy and sweet when he asked Faith if the missionary position was on the dessert menu. As a result, Faith brought him home with an eye toward inhaling helium into her otherwise deflated life.

Regrettably, Hermes snapped the hyoid bone in the front of Faith's neck. She couldn't say exactly why she had agreed to being choked during sex. She put it down to peer pressure because Hermes had assured her that, "All the kids are doing it." In any event, as Racheal gagged and turned blue, Ray was wakened from his sleep and moved toward sympathetic percussion. He banged his helmeted head against the wall in the hallway which felt very much like the cops using a door breeching tool. But it wasn't until Faith managed to scream Ray's name that he, the *safe word*, began to recite:

> *A-tisket a-tasket*
> *A green and yellow basket.*
> *I wrote a letter to my love*
> *And on the way I dropped it.*
> *I dropped it,*
> *I dropped it,*
> *And on the way I dropped it.*
> *A little boy he picked it up and put it in his pocket.*

Thereafter, Phil arrived in his wheelchair with a shotgun and a message for his daughter's assailant. "Sometimes," he said, "the yellow prick road is paved with led." For Hermes, mashed-up metaphors were the prophecies of Nostradamus, but there was nothing figurative about Phil's Remington. He pressed the knot of his clothes against his erection as though he had suddenly discovered a taste for decency. "Just so we're clear," he said, backpedalling, "this was a consensual act."

The next morning, Faith put on Phil's neck brace from the time he fell and started to build outward her disguise. In addition to her baseball cap that read Trailer Park Bitch, she wore a Team Bubba button and Old Glory sunglasses. Her firearm was a credible accessory in more ways than one as was the radio station tuned to Christian Rock. More importantly, she had used her finger to draw an alternate route on her GPS. Anyway, it was a five-hour drive to the clinic and she had already been shot at from various grassy knolls by people who believed in the sanctity of life.

On her way out the door, she found Phil sitting on the porch in his gas mask. He looked her way and said, "We didn't sell, but they own us." Effectively, Simmons, the pig folk, had built an industrial animal farm as far as the eye could see. On bad days, when the pig folk were spreading manure, Phil and Ray and Faith had red eyes, parched throats and headaches from the noise and dust and smell. Phil didn't say anything about Hermes and the neck brace. He did say, "It's worse on the Fourth of July when you can smell the barbecue and the shit at all once."

The plan was to drop Ray at the care center and then to drop Phil at the V.A. and then to start her day at the clinic. But things went south in a hurry. All the windows at the care center had their lockdown blinds drawn and there were police and emergency vehicles on Delaney and Rasmussen. Faith didn't feel comfortable talking to the police. Most cops took a dim view of her work and she would appear at the top of their list on a long night of lawless purge.

To make matters worse, the officer at her car window saw the butt of the handgun holstered at her side and drew his own. This was unusual. In any event, Faith raised her arms in the air and screamed, "I've got a permit!" In the back seat, Ray took the pulse of the situation and began knocking his helmeted head against the back of Faith's headrest. Each blow to the headrest sent shock waves through the bone fragments in her neck. While she gave her concealed gun permit to the police officer, Faith looked in the rearview mirror and exhorted her son to focus elsewhere. "Rhyme, Ray," she said. "Rhyme. Rhyme. Rhyme."

Effectively, Ray took the bait, steadied himself and read the text before his mind's eye whose prose, truth be told, sounded a little like the national anthem of North Korea:

Fifty Nifty United States from thirteen original colonies;
Fifty Nifty stars on the flag that billows so beautifully in the breeze.
Each individual state contributes a quality that is great.
Each individual state deserves a bow. We salute them now.

Back on the road, Phil bragged that his own body was an armory of pistol-packing metallurgy and none of it registered. "The military," he said, "prepares you for death and glory. And," he added, referring to the policeman, "that young pisshead would have met his maker." In any event, neither he nor Faith spoke of the bomb threat at the Care Center for Special Needs Kids, except to say that Ray would have to accompany Faith to work and Phil would have to postpone his V.A. protest and come to the clinic to take care of Ray. They would wait in a games room for volunteers and family called the House of Cards.

As per usual, Reproductive Healthcare Services was surrounded by an eco-system of anti-choice protesters, escorts, patients and security. Most of the protesters had already begun their day with prayers, leaving shallow impressions of orderly rows of knees in the dewy grass. One man, in particular, was a fixture. He was alternately known as the *prophet* for his admonitions of hellfire, Taco Bell for his obvious love of the Beef Crunchy or Dwayne, by family and friends. In any event, Dwayne wore a GoPro camera strapped to his chest and immediately hit the record button when he saw Faith exit her car in the company of Phil and Ray. He bellowed like a carnival carny and pointed a finger, "The anti-Christ is among us!"

Faith let go of Phil's wheelchair and used her own fingers to create goat horns on the top of her head. Undeterred, Dwayne said he had a few more choice words for the baby killer and more on her son. Regrettably, Faith heard *moron son* and went ballistic. Security at the front door, an African-American named Horace, corralled Faith into his 300 pound frame and whispered in her ear, "Holster-up, baby girl." And then, enigmatically, "If the five-o show, a black man die." Both the pain in her neck and Horace's plea for clemency woke her from murderous rage. She holstered her sidearm and entered the clinic.

Things did not go well. Later that morning, Faith was performing an *evacuation* when blood suddenly gushed and squirted from a torn cervix and a punctured uterus. She was closing the wounds when the building began to shake. This set off the fire alarm that sent all personnel and their patients scurrying onto the front lawn. Worse for Faith, the fire alarm had triggered the sprinkler head in her operating room, showering both her and her body apron.

She exited the building into sweltering 100 degree heat. She looked like the heroine of the horror movie, *Carrie*, after the sow blood has doused her head to toe. Behind her, to one side, were her colleagues, most of whom snacking on Fritos and Doctor Pepper. To the other side, the patients huddled, like a migratory herd. Each wore a mask associated with Guy Fawkes or the hacktivist group, *Anonymous*. This was Faith's idea. Patients were terrified of being outed and vilified.

Phil had exited the House of Cards and arrived with Ray tethered to his wheelchair with a bungee cord and hog rings. "Sons of bitches!" he screamed. These *sons of bitches* were both the protesters and those responsible for the earthquake. The oil industry had been *fracking* in dozens of counties and these were widely associated with the slipping of tectonic plates. To no one in particular, Phil said, "The oil guys don't give a shit. And the pig folk don't give a shit. And the V.A. man don't give a shit. And Uncle Sam's got a finger pointed in my direction and a thumb up his ass."

Of course, the prophet triangulated the data differently. "This is God's warning," he said, "to those who are godless!" He shook out the spit from the orange traffic cone that amplified his voice while Ray shook out snow globes. Thereafter, Phil turned his venom toward Faith and fired off an observation and a round from his Remington, metaphorically speaking, "You're a bloody mess," he said. And, "Why you gotta kill babies?"

Faith gave Phil the silent treatment on the way home. She said nothing when Phil exhorted her, like him, to sue the army for poisoning her unborn son with fire-fighting foam. Of course, they had been through all that a hundred times. Even if it were true, fifteen years of court dates and a trillion dollar military budget were the long shadow of a very bad thing.

And Faith said nothing when Phil noticed graffiti on the Henderson Overpass that read, *Fuk Amerika*. Phil rolled down the car window and screamed, "Love it or leave it!" Privately, to Ray, he whispered, "Snowflakes can't spell."

And Faith said nothing when Phil said, "Sorry."

Back home, Phil took up residence on the sofa and parked Ray beside him. They would watch video highlights of the U.S. ice hockey victory over Russia during the 1980 Winter Olympics. According to Phil, the "miracle on ice" was the biggest turning point in human history, greater than the slave trade or the Industrial Revolution. "After that," he liked to say, quoting an expression in general use during the American Civil War, "everything went to hell in a handbasket." The practised routine for both Phil and Ray was to celebrate goals from Schneider, Johnson (twice) and Eruzione by shaking a snow globe.

Meanwhile, Faith stayed in her room and started to record an audition for a podcast service. Because Phil did not, as yet, qualify for disability and Ray had aged out on one health plan and wouldn't qualify for another because of existing conditions, she was always looking to make a little extra money. This particular app released erotic-positive romance using original fiction and voice actors. It was a retro-escapist medium for those flatlining on CIG.

But things went from bad to worse lickety-split. She couldn't put her finger on it, but something had happened in the last 24 hours or 38 years to bring her to a moment of deep cognitive dissonance. Try as she may, she was unable to move her imagination into the real world. What something like erotic-positive romance might sound like *over there* became misshapen and grotesque *over here*. And the longer she tried and the greater her frustration, the more she sounded like a smoker with a stoma in her neck and a tracheostomy tube or, failing that, someone with a broken hyoid bone.

Ray heard it first and started to work himself into a tizzy at the time of Johnson's goal, his second. He smashed the snow globe called *Wow Glitter with American Eagle* on his helmeted head. The contents spilled onto the floor. Phil shrieked at the sight of the eagle and shards of glass on the carpet, "What the *hell*, Ray?" But Ray wasn't done. He then smashed *Christmas at Graceland* on his head followed by *Mickey and Minnie Go West*. Phil had never struck Ray, but the idea was the glint of a fish in deep water. And then Phil heard Faith's pornographic larynx.

    He hopped into his wheelchair and sped after his shotgun. He was convinced that Hermes, the gold-tooth standard for stranglers, had crawled into Faith's bedroom window and come with sex and vengeance on his mind. The door was locked. He would need to shoot it open, confront the assailant and extract a body, luck on his side.

    In the middle of a snow globe junkyard and dripping of water, antifreeze and particles of gold foil, Ray auto-corrected as his mother had taught him. When the first shot rang out, he had already located a nursery rhyme from a catacomb deep within his brain, accompaniment to a centuries-old *ring game* whose English version chronicled body sores on plague victims and whose American version portended apocalypse:

> *Ring around the rosy,*
> *A pocket full of posies,*
> *Ashes! Ashes!*
> *We all fall down!*

Acknowledgements

1. "Cicada"
HIGHLY COMMENDED LIST in the Manchester Fiction Prize, England, 2017
FINALIST in the Seán Ó Faoláin Short Story Prize in Cork, Ireland, 2017 (published online in *Southward* by the Munster Literature Centre)
SECOND PRIZE (of 2000+ submissions) in the Short Story Project New Beginnings Contest, New York, 2019 (published online)
FIRST RUNNER-UP for the John H. Kim Memorial Fiction Prize, published in the Raw Art Review, 2020
2. "The red-eye from *Guernica* to Pamplona"
FINALIST in The Brighton Prize, England, 2017 (published in the *Brighton Prize Anthology*)
3. "Nobody Knows How Much You Love Him"
FINALIST in the Writers' Community of Simcoe County, Short Fiction Contest in Canada, 2017
FIRST PLACE in the Bacopa Literary Review International Short Story Contest in Gainesville, Florida, 2018 (published in the *Bacopa Literary Review*)
4. "Dementia"
SECOND PLACE in the CTD Pen 2 Paper Short Story Contest in Austin, Texas, 2017
5. "Officers of Adaptation to Climate Change"
FINALIST and TOP 25 LIST (of 1000+ entries) in the Glimmer Train Press Short Fiction Contest, Portland, Oregon, 2018
LONGLIST OF FINALISTS in the Bath Short Story Award in Bath, England, 2018
LONGLIST OF FINALISTS in the Margaret River Short Story Competition in Western Australia, 2019
LONGLIST OF FINALISTS in the Flash 500 Short Story Contest, England, 2019
LONGLIST OF FINALISTS in the E.J. Brady Short Story Competition, Australia, 2019

FINALIST in the Wild Women Short Story Competition, Colorado, 2019 (published in the spring edition of the *Tulip Tree Review*)
6. "La Cuenta, por favor"
THIRD PRIZE in the Atticus Review International Flash Fiction Contest, Pennsylvania, 2018 (published in *The Atticus Review*)
7. "Empire in the Gardens of Babylon"; also, "The Astrophysical Implications of Barbecue"
FIRST PLACE in the Half and One International Short Story Prize in India, 2019 (published in the *Half And One Prize Anthology*)
8. "Head Smashed in Buffalo Jump"
SHORTLIST in the international Freefall Prose Competition in Alberta, CA, 2019
TOP FOUR in the E.J. Brady International Short Story Competition, Australia, 2019
FIRST PLACE in the short story competition at the Eden Mills Writers Festival, Ontario, Canada, 2019
RUNNER-UP for the John H. Kim Memorial Fiction Prize, Raw Art Review, Maryland, 2020
9. "Misanthropes"
SHORTLIST in the Cunningham International Short Story Contest, Surrey, England, 2019, published in the contest anthology
LONGLIST OF FINALISTS in the Flash 500 Short Story Contest, England, 2019
LONGLIST OF FINALISTS in the E.J. Brady Short Story Competition, Australia, 2019
10. "Necropsy"
LONGLIST OF FINALISTS in the E.J. Brady Short Story Competition, Australia, 2019
11. "A Night at the Oprah (sic)"
SHORTLIST OF FINALISTS (of 2800+ submissions) for the Alpine Fellowship Literary Prize, Sweden, 2019
12. "(Hogtied)"
FINALIST in the Short Fiction Competition sponsored by the Federation of British Columbia Writers, 2019
13. "1/32nd African American"
FINALIST in the Short Fiction Competition sponsored by the Federation of British Columbia Writers, 2019

14. "Dakhma"
LONGLIST OF FINALISTS for The 2019 Peter Hinchcliffe Short Fiction Award sponsored by The New Quarterly, Ontario, Canada, 2019
WINNER of the Angelo B Natoli International Short Story Award in Victoria, Australia, 2019
15. "Gloria in Excelsis Deo"
WINNER of the Two Sisters Writing and Publishing Short Story Contest, Silver City, New Mexico, anthology publication, 2020
16. "Gods, Titans and Junk"
SHORTLIST for the Into the Void Fiction Prize, Ontario, Canada, 2019
17. "Blaming Justin Bieber"
Selected for publication in the "neighbours" themed anthology by Cracked Spine Press, Texas, 2020
18. "Extinction Redux" (also called "The Wages of Misogyny")
SEMI-FINALIST for the Meridian Short Prose Prize in Virginia, U.S.A., 2019
WINNER in the New Millennium/Musepaper flash fiction contest in Tennessee, U.S.A., anthology publication in 2020
19. "The Brief Sad Tale of Ping Pong" (also called "Ping Pong in Bangkok")
SHORTLIST for the Neilma Sydney Short Story Prize from Overland, Australia, 2020

Other Books by Dean Gessie

Guantanamo Redux, Anaphora Literary Press, Brownsville, Texas, 2016.
A Brief History of Summer Employment, Anaphora Literary Press, Brownsville, Texas, 2017.
TrumpeterVille, Anaphora Literary Press, Brownsville, Texas, 2017.